Kindness of Strangers

A Medieval Fiction novel about miracles, Friendship and acceptance During a time of war

Marina Pacheco

Marina Pacheco

Copyright © 2020 Marina Pacheco

The right of Marina Pacheco to be identified as the author of the Work has been asserted by her in accordance with the Copyright, Designs and Patents Act 1988.

All rights reserved.

No part of this publication may be reproduced, or transmitted in any form or by any means, electronic or otherwise, without written permission from the author.

This is a work of fiction. Names, characters, places and incidents are used fictitiously. Any resemblance to actual events, or persons, living or dead, is coincidental.

contents

1. Chapter 1   1

2. Chapter 2   10

3. Chapter 3   20

4. Chapter 4   29

5. Chapter 5   42

6. Chapter 6   55

7. Chapter 7   65

8. Chapter 8   72

9. Chapter 9   80

10. Chapter 10   89

11. Chapter 11   97

12. Chapter 12   103

13. Chapter 13   112

14. Chapter 14   122

15. Chapter 15   129

16. Chapter 16   144

17. Chapter 17   152

18. Chapter 18   161

19. Chapter 19   170

20. Background to the book   175

21. Glossary   176

Get all my short stories for FREE!   178

Also By   179

About Author   184

CHapter 1

G alen prayed to God to ease the agony he was in as he clung on to the back of the cart that bumped its way down the road at little more than a walking pace. The wheels seemed to have an unerring ability to find every pothole. It sent a solid thump through his body that wrenched at his gut and left him so nauseous it was all he could do not to throw up.

To distract himself, he switched to praying to his favourite saints: Cuthbert and Bede. He felt a special affinity for both. First, because they were Anglo-Saxons like him. Second, because they had also been monks and men of learning.

Transcribing Bede's Life of Cuthbert had inspired Galen. He hoped one day he'd be able to pen books half as good. So now he mulled over the life of Cuthbert and tried to derive lessons to help him weather this journey.

When that failed to distract him sufficiently, Galen forced his eyes open to watch the countryside roll by. He couldn't decide which method helped the most. Neither did much to ease the pain.

To be fair, there wasn't much to see. The land was as flat as a board and marshy. Pools of water filled with croaking frogs broke up the vast stretches of reedbeds.

Great clouds of birds rose from the rushes in a clatter of wings, disturbed by some unknown force, perhaps an otter out foraging.

Although it wasn't discernible to the human eye, at times they must have passed over higher ground because copses of silver birch, alder and willow had managed to put down roots in this drier soil. These little clusters of trees provided some welcome shade in the heat of the day. They did nothing for the midges that hovered like a miniature army of black dots and attacked as only the most persistent warriors could.

On rare occasions, they'd pass a hamlet either on higher ground or land reclaimed from the marsh, with an intricate network of ditches around it. They were usually so small there was only a sprinkling of five or six houses. Their walls were dark since the daub used to waterproof them was stained with the black earth of the marsh. The roofs were thicker too, as thatch was abundant.

Although it wasn't the rolling landscape of home, this marshland had become familiar to him from his years at the Abbey of Yarmwick. Galen had spent three years in that vast Benedictine institution that had seemed strange when he'd first arrived as a novice, but now was familiar and comforting.

The people harvesting their crops, fishing and tending their livestock would stop to watch them pass. Some even came alongside to chat and find out more about the strangers travelling through their land. Galen accepted their curiosity, for he was an inquiring man himself.

If it weren't for his shyness, he, too, might have approached such a peculiar group of travellers. Their most striking difference was the canopy on the cart, stretched tight over a framework of struts. His father had ordered it made to protect Galen from the sun and the rain, but it was surely a unique sight.

Today, they had a change in the weather from the days of sunshine so far this summer. Thick clouds were gathering overhead, and Galen expected it might rain soon. The oppressive weight of the air suggested they might even be in for a thunderstorm.

'How are you faring?' Alcuin asked as he leaned down over the mule he was riding and examined Galen.

Galen forced a smile and hoped that his knuckles, white from gripping the side of the cart, didn't give him away.

'I'm fine,' he managed, but doubted that Alcuin believed him.

Still, Alcuin gave an accepting nod.

'We won't go very much further, don't worry.'

'At this rate, we'll never get to Lundenburh,' Galen ground out through gritted teeth. 'What will the king think of us then?'

What would the king think of them at all? It was astonishing to Galen that he and Alcuin had been summoned to produce a book for the king. Galen felt tremendously honoured to have been chosen, while the whole idea also terrified him. He wasn't sure how he would cope with the fierce ealdormen and thanes that surrounded the king.

'Don't worry, we have plenty of time to get to court,' Alcuin said as he urged his mule forward.

Galen would have given anything to stop. But, despite Alcuin's relaxed attitude, they were later than expected getting to the king's hall. Galen sensed Alcuin was worried about that, even if he didn't voice his concerns. So, even though it caused him pain, Galen thought it would be better to keep going. This ordeal would only end when they finally reached Lundenburh.

The sound of Alcuin's voice drifted over to Galen. He was having a word with the carter, to either slow down or stop for a rest. They had been on the road for so long, a camaraderie had formed between Alcuin and Niclas that broke down some of the difference in their ranks.

Galen sometimes felt a bit left out, but then blamed himself for that. He was too shy, and he was ill and at the back of the cart. Little wonder Alcuin had taken to chatting to the carter instead.

They were going so slowly that there wasn't much noise from the wooden wheels. Alcuin, though, obviously hadn't realised that Galen could hear him and Niclas talking. Galen didn't mind. Sometimes their conversation helped to divert him from his discomfort.

'What's worrying you, Niclas?' Galen heard Alcuin ask.

'I'm just looking out for vikings. The harvests are nearly all in and that's when they start their raiding,' Niclas said.

This news sent a spasm of fear through Galen. His eldest brother, Willnoth, had been killed in a viking raid. Were they actually at risk from raiders? Or was the carter being overly concerned about nothing?

Then Galen remembered with a nervous start that his father had urged them to make haste to Lundenburh and get there before the harvest was over. Galen had assumed that was so they did not keep the king waiting. Now he feared vikings might have been the reason.

'Vikings? Aren't we a little too far inland for that?'

Alcuin's tone was that of someone trying to jolly another out of their fears.

'There are rivers all around in this wetland, and that's all it takes,' Niclas said. 'Those damned viking ships have such shallow bottoms they can get right up a river. It's one reason we'll be skirting around Grantabrycge. It's a Danish settlement.'

Galen knew all about Grantabrycge. It was one of many Danish settlements occupied by marauding vikings over the last hundred years. It worried him that Niclas feared them so much that he was going to skirt past one of their towns. As far as he was aware, the settled Danes had all become Christians. They were therefore at as much risk from their fellow countrymen's raids as the rest of the people of Enga-lond.

'But we have seen no sign of vikings,' Alcuin said.

'No, just well-fortified burhs.'

'Well, yes, there is that, but nothing more. Nothing burned down. We'll be fine.'

'Still,' Niclas muttered, 'it would have been good to have a couple of armed guards. If not to protect us from the vikings, then to keep robbers at bay.'

'If Ealdorman Hugh didn't give us a guard, it was because he didn't think we'd need one. Besides, you look like a powerful fighter and so am I. We'll see off any rogues.'

'What of him?' Niclas said.

Galen guessed that he was the one being referred to.

'I've seen him stab someone to keep him at bay. He'll try his best,' Alcuin said.

It warmed Galen's heart that Alcuin thought him competent enough to mention something like that. But his penknife was the only weapon he had, and that wouldn't be any use against a viking's spear or axe. Alcuin was right though, he would use it if he had to.

'But he isn't up to it, is he?' Niclas said. 'This journey is sapping his strength. Every evening he's more tired than the night before.'

'Aye, it's hard for him, but he doesn't complain.'

'I've also noticed that.'

'What did Hugh's people make of him?'

Galen shut his eyes tight, as if that would help block out Niclas's words. He wasn't ready to hear what the people in his father's burh thought of him.

'They didn't know what to think,' Niclas said. 'We all remember when he was raped, though. Thoughts weren't so charitable then. People claimed they'd seen him up to all sorts, but they were lies. I remember he was just very quiet. You didn't see him around much. So when it happened, well, nobody blamed his lordship for throwing him out.

'Then, after Septimus killed the other men, it got people to wondering and remembering. That's when they started talking about how Master Galen had done this or that kind thing for them. And he is a good man, isn't he?' Niclas said. 'I mean, you wouldn't be so protective of him if he wasn't.'

'I suppose not,' Alcuin said with a laugh. 'Actually, I like Galen because he's clever, and he's a damned good scribe. I can forgive a man almost anything, as long as he makes my work look as good as Galen's writing does.'

Galen had long ago heard that it was painful to overhear people talking about you. But while Niclas and Alcuin's conversation had him squirming, it was worth it to hear Alcuin praise his work. It made him feel like he'd earned his place as the scribe Alcuin preferred for his illustrations.

'You two are an excellent match then,' Niclas said. 'I heard you did all those beautiful pictures in the new book of hours.'

'You've seen them?' Alcuin said in surprise.

'His lordship lined us all up in the church and showed it to us. He was ever so proud of it.'

'I'm glad to hear it.'

Galen was too. His father had mentioned showing the book to the king, but he'd not told Galen about the rest. It made him rethink their last encounter when Hugh had told him he had the potential for greatness.

It was a surprise to hear that from his father, who'd never had time for him when he was growing up. Galen wasn't sure whether Hugh was being sincere or merely kind. Now Galen was starting to believe he actually meant it.

'Ho there!' someone shouted from behind, and Galen forced his eyes open again.

A man was hurrying up the track towards them, emerging from amongst the tall reeds. His clothes were more colourful than that of a local. They were more ornate than most people's, in fact, with an embroidered edging to a red tunic. They looked like they'd belonged to a richer man once and were faded and tattered now, but still spoke of past grandeur. More interestingly, he carried a harp over his shoulder.

There was only one type of person who wandered from town to town with a musical instrument, and that was a gleeman. It was always a source of excitement when one showed up at the burh. He brought with him a great storehouse of songs, riddles and sagas.

The best of these men were superb showmen. They could hold an audience's attention so tightly that his father's hall would fall silent to listen. Then the only sounds remaining were the voice of the gleeman and the crackling of the fire.

As he got closer, Galen noticed the man's unkempt greying hair and beard. His nose was red and a fine network of blood vessels covered his face, indicating he was a heavy drinker. That wasn't surprising either. It seemed to be a fairly common trait for gleemen.

'Yes, traveller?' Alcuin said, dropping back to talk to the man.

'My good monk,' the man said, bowing, 'I am Swidhelm, a gleeman of some renown. May I join your company so we may travel together in greater safety? I hear that the risk of attack from vikings in this area is high, especially at this time of the year.'

Galen got the impression that the man hadn't noticed him. Alcuin also didn't look towards him, so he continued to go unremarked.

'You are welcome to join us, but if it's vikings you fear, I doubt we would be much to deter them.'

'I'm afraid you are right,' Swidhelm said. 'All the same, there is safety in numbers, is there not?'

Alcuin nodded and said, 'Come up to the front of the cart and I'll introduce you to Niclas.'

'Ah, the carter,' Swidhelm said, beaming up at Alcuin. 'Perhaps he will allow me to ride beside him. I have travelled far lately and my legs ache. And then you must tell me all about your fascinating equipage. I have never seen such an interesting vehicle before, with this canopy. Would it not have been easier to lay a canvas over the top of your goods to keep them dry?'

'Perhaps,' Alcuin said, as he dismounted and finally looked at Galen, his eyebrow raised in query.

He was asking for permission to make an introduction. Part of Galen wanted to remain anonymous and unnoticed. But Swidhelm had already shown himself to be an inquisitive man. He'd find it even odder to discover Galen later, so he nodded acceptance.

'The canopy is for my fellow monk, Brother Galen,' Alcuin said, waving his hand in Galen's direction.

The gleeman's eyebrows rose in surprise as he looked Galen over. He supposed he must look strange, huddled as he was at the back.

'Well, well, it's a pleasure and an honour to meet you both,' Swidhelm said, executing another deep bow.

CHAPTER 2

Alcuin's initial assessment of Swidhelm as overly curious proved correct. No sooner had he pulled himself up onto the cart to sit beside Niclas than he started on a barrage of questions: where they were from, where they were going, and what they did, being the main ones.

Alcuin gave Niclas a warning look that he hoped led the man to understand he should hold his tongue.

'Brother Galen and I are from the Abbey of Yarmwick. I'm an illustrator and Galen is a scribe. Niclas is from Thorpe Parva, where Galen's father is the ealdorman. We are heading to Lundenburh to work on a commission for the king.'

'Ah, I see,' Swidhelm said. 'A commission for the king. That's grand, very grand indeed. But I think there is even more to this story, if I'm not mistaken. Young Brother Galen seems rather sickly to undertake such a long trip.'

Alcuin gave Niclas another even more severe warning look.

'Galen is struggling with the journey, that is all.'

There was no way Alcuin was going to mention what had happened to Galen, to someone who was both nosy and chatty.

'Tell us about yourself, Swidhelm. Where do you hail from?'

'Ah, here and there,' Swidhelm said, waving his hand to encompass all. 'Of late I have journeyed from the west. I spent some time among the Wealisc and then kept going east until I found myself back at the sea. But as there are more vikings about of late, I thought it prudent to head back inland.'

'I told you there were vikings about,' Niclas muttered.

He crossed himself several times and cast a fearful glance at the river that their path was following.

The water was grey, and ripples formed on its surface with the gathering wind. It looked gloomy and reflected the gleeman's ominous mood. It was just as well Galen couldn't hear them. Then a great gust of wind rattled through the reeds and buffeted the travellers. It even made Alcuin anxious.

'It's a portent,' Niclas said.

'Nonsense! It's just a storm. It will blow over in no time,' Alcuin said, as he examined the dark clouds massing overhead.

A crack of lightning lit everything in preternatural brightness. Then a bang of thunder shook the earth and the heavens opened and poured out buckets of rain. Whether or not it was a portent, Alcuin didn't fancy getting wet.

'Dear God, have mercy.'

Alcuin swung himself out of the saddle, hitched Goat the mule to a back post of the cart and, with a hop, cleared the backboard and landed beside Galen.

'I hope you don't mind if I join you,' he said cheerfully.

Galen forced his eyes open and barely managed a smile before he closed them again.

'Galen, are you alright?' Alcuin said, and his heart filled with alarm.

Galen was sweating even though the rain had cooled the air. He was paler than usual and had both arms wrapped about himself as he gave a slight nod.

'Galen, talk to me!'

Alcuin was afraid that his friend was in so much pain that even speech was impossible.

'I'm fine,' Galen said through clenched teeth.

'No.' Alcuin leaned out of the cart and shouted, 'Niclas, pull over. We're stopping for the day.'

'What, already? We've barely got going and really, Brother Alcuin, the rain won't make travel impossible.'

'And what of the vikings?' Swidhelm shouted.

'Considering the strength of the rain, any vikings are probably also hunkered down.' Alcuin was annoyed that Swidhelm had mentioned vikings because Galen would worry about it. 'Anyway, Galen needs to rest.'

'Out here?' Niclas held his hand out, palm upward, gathering the rain. 'Wouldn't it be better to head to the little hamlet down the track? It isn't far.'

'No!' Swidhelm snapped, and then looked surprised at his own abrupt intervention.

He took a deep breath, about to embark on a host of reasons, but Alcuin didn't have the patience or inclination to hear him out.

'We'll stay here in the cart. We'll be fine. I don't dare move Galen for the moment.'

'That bad huh?' Niclas pulled the cart half off the road into a newly cleared circle of chopped down trees. 'Do you need anything from me?'

'Just some water if you can manage it.'

Niclas looked up into the rain with a grin.

'I can do that. After which I'll take myself off to some shelter. There's got to be somewhere I can sit without the sky dumping its contents on me.'

'I'll shout if I need you,' Alcuin said and pulled his head back into the cart.

Galen hadn't even reacted to them stopping. So Alcuin decided drastic measures were called for. He searched through his belongings for Brother Benesing's powerful medicine. He'd just unearthed it when Niclas arrived with a bowl half full of water.

'I'll unhitch the mule and take it to shelter. There's no sense in leaving it in harness, is there?' Niclas said.

'None at all. Take Goat with you as well, please. We aren't going anywhere. What's happened to Swidhelm?'

'He's still with us,' Niclas said. 'I thought he might take off, what with us stopping. But the cart is obviously more attractive than running away from potential danger.'

'Watch what you say and keep an eye on him at all times. I don't trust him.'

'Right you are,' Niclas said, and then ran off to find shelter for himself.

Alcuin watched him go before he measured out a dose of medicine into the water and held it to Galen's lips.

'Here, drink this.'

'What is it?' Galen muttered, his eyes shut fast.

'Something to make you feel better. Now, don't argue with me, just drink it.'

'It's that sleeping draft of my uncle's,' Galen said as he came up for air from his first sip. 'I don't need it.'

'I'll be the judge of that. Now drink up.'

Alcuin tipped the remaining contents of the bowl into Galen's mouth. He would not put up with any arguments. In fact, he was annoyed at Galen for allowing things to come to such a pass. Although, knowing his friend, he might not have realised how bad it was getting. Nor would he be willing to put a stop to their journey merely for his own comfort.

Alcuin watched as the drug took effect and Galen's arms slipped from his waist and hung loosely beside him. This was the sign to get Galen to lie down. It was an operation that would have been too tricky when he was so rigidly tense before.

'What are you doing?' Galen muttered as Alcuin gently pulled him along the floor and lay him down.

'I'm making you comfortable.'

Then Alcuin pulled Galen's black hood up over his head to keep him warm and protect him from the splashes of rain that slanted in under the canopy.

'In the cart?'

'I daren't risk moving you any further.'

'Oh,' Galen said, fast losing interest as the drug's lethargy spread through him and infected his mind.

Alcuin was thankful for that. It meant he wouldn't have an argument. Galen was usually willing to go along with anything Alcuin suggested, but not if it meant slowing them down. Such was his anxiety to obey the king's summons. At least with this powerful medicine, Galen even lost the inclination to do that.

Alcuin watched him closely though, praying he hadn't started to bleed. He couldn't see any sign of it. But as his experience of what brought the bleeding on wasn't extensive, he couldn't relax until a couple of hours had passed.

By this time Galen had subsided into a deep and sonorous sleep which Beelzebub himself couldn't rouse him from. This thought alarmed Alcuin. Had he overdone the dose? No, he'd measured it exactly as Brother Benesing had told him to do.

He remembered Galen had a similar reaction to the medicine at his father's burh. But there he'd been left in his mother's care. Alcuin had never sat with Galen after he'd been medicated and seen the full effect of the drug.

Alcuin had never realised how much Galen's face reflected the pain he was in. Now it was less pinched. His lips weren't pulled tight, either, making his mouth white about the edges. As the rain drummed down on their roof, Alcuin wondered how much pain Galen was normally in when the additional strain of travelling was removed.

It had to be great, considering the glove Galen wore on his left hand to prevent him from digging his nails into the flesh of his palm. Alcuin supposed he only didn't do the same to his right hand because he needed it for writing. It had to take great discipline to keep his hand moving so smoothly from inkhorn to page, forming those perfect letters.

Alcuin woke when somebody shook his shoulder. It took a while to assimilate the fact that it was dark and Niclas was grinning at him by the pale flickering light of an oil lamp.

'Do either of you want any food?' Niclas asked.

'Did I sleep throughout the day?'

'Yes indeed. Looks like Master Galen wasn't the only one who needed a rest.'

'I have to check on him.'

Alcuin pushed himself upright and shook the lethargy from his mind. Galen was still asleep, but not snoring as loudly as before. A slight crease had also appeared between his eyebrows. It looked like the drug was wearing off. But a whispered calling of Galen's name didn't elicit a response.

The rain had given way to a crisp, clear night, so Alcuin was happy to leave the cramped confines of the cart and join Niclas for a bite of food. He was less pleased to see the gleeman was still with them.

'Since you've been sleeping all day, how do you feel about taking the first watch?' Niclas asked.

'Fair enough.' Alcuin had no intention of leaving Swidhelm to take a watch unobserved by any other, so he was willing to do the entire night himself. 'I take it you two stood guard throughout the day?'

'It wasn't difficult,' Niclas said. 'Swidhelm says that the track we're on leads to a couple more hamlets on the river. But most of the other traffic keeps to the main road, so there wasn't much to see.'

'Alright, then I should have a quiet night. You two sleep. I'll keep watch and tomorrow you might like to drop in on one of the hamlets and buy some food.'

'We're not going on tomorrow?'

'No. I daren't move Galen yet.'

Alcuin watched Swidhelm as he spoke and noted a spark of interest in his eye. He also said nothing about heading off on his own. Alcuin couldn't really believe that he'd want to delay his journey for another day.

Then again, here he had protection, free food and the chance to hitch a ride, which could explain everything. Alcuin had his doubts, though. He didn't know why, but Swidhelm worried him.

'Brother Galen is taking it hard,' Niclas said, shaking his head.

'We've been on the road longer than the trip to his father's burh. He's bound to be even more exhausted than that first time, and it took him a week to recover from that.'

'God's Bones! This is going to be a very long journey.'

Since Alcuin had long ago come to the same conclusion and he didn't want to fuel Swidhelm's curiosity, he said no more.

'Goodnight then,' Niclas said.

He put his hand on Swidhelm's shoulder and led the man away. Alcuin watched them settle beside a small fire under the spreading branches of a willow. It had such a dense canopy it looked like it may have kept the rain off the two men.

Then Alcuin stretched and, now that his eyes had adjusted to the dark, looked around the clearing. It was dotted about with freshly sawn stumps. There were also drag marks where the larger boughs and the main trunks had been pulled out.

A pile of logs still stood by the edge of the road. No doubt they'd be collected shortly by whoever had cut everything down. The stumps provided a convenient place to sit, but they were less useful for anyone keeping watch.

So Alcuin looked around for a good vantage point, preferably a dry one. That was probably a vain hope. He could hear a soft pitter patter of dripping leaves. Wherever he went, he was going to get wet.

Alcuin hitched his robes up around his waist and clambered along the trunk of a fallen willow that hung out over the river. He bumped one of the upright branches and released a shower of icy droplets. They somehow all found the gap around his neck and slid down his back.

Alcuin gave an uncomfortable wriggle and pressed his clothes down to dry himself. Then he continued along the ridged trunk to near the end where the tree curved downwards, dipping into the river. From this position, he could see faint dots of light both upstream and downstream. The Ouse, they called this river, according to Niclas.

Since it was marshland, the Ouse didn't meander neatly through a valley. This river broke into multiple channels. It sprawled about and rejoined with its many tributaries over and over again. So they not only followed one river but frequently came to points that needed to be forded as another bit of the river crossed their path.

Alcuin's gaze remained fixed on the flickering lights from the hamlets. They were barely visible in this dark and wet landscape; tiny islands of civilisation in a dark and uncaring world. He sat with his legs straddling the main trunk of the tree, leaned against an upright branch and looked up at the stars. He hadn't done that in a long time. Not since he was a boy, and certainly not since he'd become a monk.

The silvery-white of the stars in the velvet black of the night was a perfect contrast to the flickering golden lights of human habitation. Alcuin leaned back and whiled away the time planning another composition for the king's book of hours.

Chapter 3

A high-pitched scream wrenched Alcuin from his musing. He looked about, convinced it came from right amongst them. It was dawn and a pale mist clung to the river.

Then another scream as a clash of weapons carried to him on the cool dawn air. Two sinister dragon-headed longboats rose out of the mist near the hamlet downstream. Vikings! They'd set two fishing boats ablaze, and a third was sinking. A column of smoke rose into the air from where Alcuin guessed the houses were.

'God preserve us,' Alcuin gasped as he scrambled out of the tree.

He prayed he didn't appear as a silhouette in the fast-brightening dawn as he ran to Niclas and Swidhelm. They were two huddled masses curled under their capes beside a long-dead fire.

Alcuin shook Niclas violently by the shoulder a

nd whispered, 'Get up, man. Hurry! There are viking raiders on the river,' while he kicked Swidhelm's slumbering form.

'Devil take it!' Niclas gasped as he threw back his cape and scrambled to his feet, his dagger already drawn. 'What do we do now?'

'You hitch the mule up to the cart and we ride like the wind.'

'It will never work,' Niclas whispered. 'It rained all day yesterday. The ground will be muddy and the cart will stick. We have to ride out.'

'We can't get Galen onto a mule.'

'We have to!' Swidhelm hissed, leaping to his feet. 'Those vikings give no quarter. If they catch you, they'll kill you and your little monk friend. They have no love for our religion.'

'We have no choice. He has to ride.' Niclas was so frightened he was jumping out of his skin. 'And we have to go now. Those vikings spread out like wildfire when they land.'

'Alright, gather the mules. I'll get Galen.' Alcuin ran to the cart and pulled the backboard away. 'Come on, Galen,' he said as he grabbed his friend under the arms and dragged him out into the cool morning air.

'Huh... what?' Galen was tipped into a nightmare where he was being dragged out of his bed by Septimus to be raped. He struggled against the iron grip that was pulling him out into the dawn air and realised it was Alcuin. 'What are you doing?' Galen cried as he landed hard on the ground and tried to get back up.

'Shhh, make no sound,' Alcuin whispered into his ear. 'There are vikings on the river. We have to get away from here.'

'Vikings!'

A tremor of terror shot through Galen and his legs caved in. This was no time to give in to fear, and he fought to regain control and get himself upright. Alcuin made it harder, with his arms about Galen, dragging him away from the cart.

'Where are we going?' Galen asked, dazed, terrified and confused.

'We have to ride out. There's too much mud for the cart,' Alcuin hissed as he pulled Galen to where Niclas was throwing a saddle onto a mule.

'I can't get up there.'

'You have to, we–' Alcuin cut off. They could hear voices, men shouting, and it was getting closer. Alcuin leapt into the saddle and said, 'Niclas, quickly, help him up,' as he grabbed Galen by the shoulders and heaved to get him up in front of him.

Niclas pushed from below and Galen clutched at Alcuin's robe and pulled himself into a sitting position.

'I have you,' Alcuin muttered and wrapped his arms around Galen as he took hold of the reins. 'Let's go.'

Galen realised he had no choice. If he was to get away from the vikings he had to risk a ride which would aggravate his injury. He wound his fingers into the mule's short, rough mane for something to hang on to and prayed to God for strength and for Him to get everybody safely away.

'Hurry!' Swidhelm hissed.

He was already on the cart mule and looking like he might set off without Niclas. The carter flung himself up onto the mule, and the two of them jogged off down the track as fast as they could.

'Hold tight,' Alcuin murmured and urged Goat into motion.

'Dear God, protect us,' Galen whispered as he heard men's voices and the tramp of feet.

The vikings were on the move. The mules, sensing the fear in their riders, needed no encouragement to break into a gallop. This was too much for Galen. The sudden lurch brought on a spasm of the most exquisite pain.

Galen doubled over, wrenching himself out of Alcuin's arms. He fell to the ground, rolled over and writhed in agony. He put his arm in his mouth, biting it to make no sound and to distract from the rest.

He was dimly aware of cursing. Then Alcuin leapt down and ran to Galen. Niclas and the gleeman were either unaware or unwilling to stop their headlong flight and vanished down the path.

'Galen, get up!' Alcuin breathed. 'For God's sake, man, we have to get away from here. You know what the vikings think of us. You know what they do to monks.'

'No,' Galen gasped through gritted teeth, 'I can't.'

'You have no choice. They'll torture you and kill you.'

'The ride will kill me too.'

'Please Galen, there's no time to argue,' Alcuin said as he reached to grab his friend.

The fear in Alcuin's eyes nearly sent Galen into a panic and then, suddenly, he knew what he had to do. He couldn't save himself, but he could save Alcuin. Galen ripped his small penknife out of his sleeve and held it to his own throat.

'You go.'

'Are you mad?'

'You have no time and I'll hold you back. Go now or I kill myself and take away the decision.'

'I can help you up again.'

'Don't you come anywhere near me. I can't let you overwhelm me and disarm me,' Galen said, the knife pressed hard against his throat.

'Can't I at least–'

'Go! There's no time!'

Galen was frantic, but also in deadly earnest. He would kill himself before he allowed Alcuin to come near him. Alcuin must have realised it too. He spun round in frustration, made to come back to Galen, saw Galen press the knife harder against his throat and gave an accepting nod.

'I'll get help. We'll rescue you.'

'Just go!'

Alcuin's mule was already in motion as he swung himself onto its back. Galen watched in case he changed his mind, but Alcuin didn't even glance back as he galloped away.

Galen wanted nothing more than to curl himself into a little ball and wail from the pain. But he forced himself to stay still and wait till he was sure Alcuin wasn't coming back. He listened too, straining his ears. The sound of fighting was definitely getting closer.

Some small part of him hadn't given in completely. He had to do what he could to keep away from the vikings. He wanted to die in his own way, not being slowly torn apart by marauders.

Galen pushed himself onto his hands and knees and fought the pain and nausea threatening to overwhelm him. He was bleeding, and it was bad, worse than it had ever been before.

It was the reason he'd resisted Alcuin. There was no point in trying to run. He was going to die anyway.

With a great effort, Galen lifted his head and, blinking to clear his fractured vision, he looked around. There was nowhere to hide. Featureless countryside stretched away to either side.

Then the corner of his eye caught their cart. It would attract the vikings, but there was a pile of logs beside it. Maybe he could hide there.

Galen tried to push himself to his feet, but it was impossible. The pain brought him to his knees on his first attempt. So he crawled through the mud, his habit growing heavier as it got more sodden and dragged at him. It hooked on his knees and pulled tight around the back of his neck on every crawl forward.

'Please God, help me,' Galen sobbed.

He pulled the habit up, whimpering with the pain and struggling at the cloth till frustration at his weak, useless fingers made him want to shriek with panic. He fell forward as the habit came free. Then he crawled past the cart, certain the vikings would be upon him at any moment.

He made it to the pile of logs and dragged himself into the gap between them. It was right by the side of the road. It would be safer if he could get deeper into the small copse of trees, but he couldn't. His strength was spent.

Galen lay face down for a moment, trying to catch his breath. Then he rolled himself onto his side, pulled his feet in under his mud-saturated robe and prayed. God would always be with him. At least he knew that, and it brought him comfort.

It felt strange to think this was where he was going to die, but of that, he was certain. He'd always believed his injury would carry him off, but he'd not thought it would be so soon. His only regret was that he was going to die alone and he wouldn't see his family again.

The sound of a scream broke through his thoughts. It was high-pitched, as from a child, and it was coming towards him. A girl tripped, her cry cut short, and landed face-first right beside Galen.

As if in a dream, he reached out, grabbed her dress, pulled her into the gap beside him and threw his cloak over the two of them. The girl kicked, struggling against this sudden imprisonment.

'Shhh!' Galen gasped as he clapped one hand over her mouth and wrapped the other tight about her.

He prayed she'd stop wriggling because he didn't have the strength to keep her from breaking free otherwise. The girl stared in terror at him, then subsided, trembling beside him.

Three vikings ran past the logs and stopped as they spotted the cart. They were big men with shaggy beards and two with their hair flying about them in an unkempt mess. The third was wearing a helmet with a slight point to its domed top. A metal bar was welded to the front to protect his nose. They were each carrying circular shields with a red and white pattern painted on them. Their tunics hung open in the casual manner of the Danes and they were wearing impressive golden torques. Two were holding blood-smeared spears. The third, the one with the helmet, had a battle axe.

There was some discussion around the cart. Galen couldn't make out what they were saying because their dialect was thick and difficult. Two of the men laughed at what the axeman said as they looked about. It didn't look like they were bothered about finding the girl, Galen thought, as he closed his eyes to slits, watching. He wondered how long it would be until they were spotted.

The axeman slashed at the canopy of the cart and dragged the covering off to get at the contents more easily. One of the spearmen climbed inside and started tossing everything onto the road. They weren't impressed by what they saw. They barely glanced at the vellum and inks they threw out into the mud. They did like the gold leaf, though, and the axeman tucked that into his shirt.

They looked about a little more, then turned and shouted to someone who, Galen guessed, must be approaching. These new men gathered about the cart when they arrived, stepping on the vellum scattered in the mud. Despite the desperate position he was in, Galen winced to see this barbarism.

The band of men grew to about thirty, and Galen wondered why they hadn't spotted him and the girl yet. He was dimly aware that she was clutching his robe but, aside from that, barely making a sound. Her breathing was high and fast in his ear.

The vikings burst out laughing at some joke and set off down the road, heading in the direction Alcuin had taken. Galen prayed they wouldn't find his friends. Alcuin, the gleeman and Niclas were no match for so many men and, aside from Niclas, the other two weren't fighters.

Galen listened until the sound of the vikings had died away. Now all he could hear was the wind through the leaves of the trees. Everything else was still. It was what often happened after a battle. Even the animals hid and went silent when men went to war.

Galen did not know how much time passed, but the girl didn't move, although her breathing became more even. He wondered what she would do next. Galen could do nothing for her. He could no longer move.

He was still bleeding, and his limbs were heavy and immobile. There was a buzzing in his ears and everything had grown fuzzy. Darkness was creeping in around the edges, although he was certain it was still early.

With the growing lethargy came a blessed detachment. He no longer cared about what was happening. He could watch it in distant interest, as even the pain ebbed away.

CHapTer 4

Alcuin urged Goat onwards, sick and shaky at having left Galen behind and fighting his desire to turn around and force Galen onto the mule. He didn't have time. Now he was determined to catch Niclas and Swidhelm. He was furious with the men for having deserted them. If only they'd stayed, they might have been able to get Galen back onto the mule.

His sensible side told him it would have been impossible. Galen didn't have the strength to stay on a mule, even if they had held him. But he dreaded to think what would happen to his friend when the vikings found him.

Then again, what could he do? The vikings were still out there and he, Niclas and the gleeman wouldn't be able to fight them off alone. It might only be him at that. He still hadn't caught up with the other two. Just then, Niclas came into sight. He'd dismounted and was trying to run while dragging his limping mule by the reins. Swidhelm was running ahead, already having given up on his companion in his need to escape.

Alcuin kicked Goat harder and closed the gap.

'Leave the animal man, we have no time!'

'I can't. His lordship will kill me if I lose his mule,' Niclas said, although he was jumpy with fear.

'And he won't mind that you left his son behind, will he?'

Niclas turned white as he noticed Alcuin was alone. 'Oh God!' he moaned. 'He'll finish me for certain. What was I thinking?'

'No time to worry about that now. We have to get to the nearest burh and warn the residents. If we're lucky, we'll be able to help them fight the vikings off, get back to the cart and find Galen.'

'Do you think so?' Niclas said with the look of a man snatching at a last, vain straw.

Alcuin didn't, but he had neither the heart nor the time to say so.

'Come on!'

He jabbed his heels into his mule's sides and took off down the road. Niclas let go of his animal and followed, running full tilt but unable to keep up with Goat.

'Wait, wait for me,' Swidhelm said, breaking into a run as Alcuin thundered past.

Alcuin felt even less sympathy for him than he did for Niclas. He prayed they were near a burh and prayed even harder that it was well fortified.

In this, God answered his prayers. As he shot out of yet another copse of trees, a compact but impressively tall wooden fortress appeared on the slight rise before him. The river looped its way around half of it, forming a natural moat. It was built on the only higher ground for miles around. Even so, it was hardly much of a slope for Goat to charge up.

'Halt! Who goes there?' a tall blond guard shouted as Alcuin barrelled towards him.

Another guard joined him, and the two blocked Alcuin's access with their crossed spears.

He pulled up his exhausted, almost finished mule and said, 'I'm Brother Alcuin of Yarmwick. We are fleeing vikings. They've attacked the hamlet downriver.'

'Vikings!' the man spat and made a sign of the cross to ward off evil. 'How do I know I can trust you?'

'What reason do I have to lie to you?' Alcuin shouted. 'Besides, I'm a monk and I had to leave one of my brothers behind. I need somebody to come and help me find him.'

'If you left him in countryside with vikings around, he'll be dead by now,' the blond guard said.

Alcuin wanted to shake him out of his disbelief and order him to move. Then the stockiest, most muscular man Alcuin had ever seen emerged from the shadows.

'Did you say vikings?' he asked.

'Yes, two longboats,' Alcuin said, looking the man up and down.

He was swarthy, with a heavy gold torque around his neck and a long dark beard that ended in a plait tied with a blue knotted cord.

'Dear God, Albreda!' the man said, turning pale. 'Albreda was visiting her aunt. You, monk, when was the attack?'

'It's now. We grabbed our mules and fled the moment we saw them.'

'We?' the muscular man said, making a point of looking beyond Alcuin.

'My fellow monk and two others. They were on another mule, but it went lame. They'll get here soon. As will the vikings. They'll be on their way here too.'

'Aye,' the man said, looking Alcuin over. 'I'm Hasculf, the shire reeve of this place. Did you notice the size of the longboats?'

'The... the size?'

The question threw Alcuin, but he still tried to remember what he'd seen in case it was of use.

'They have different sized boats,' Hasculf said. 'Some only hold twenty warriors; others can hold as many as a hundred. You see why that intelligence is important?'

'Yes.' Alcuin used all his artistic observational skills to force himself to remember. 'They weren't that big, not so big that they'd hold a hundred men.'

'Let's hope you're right. You have a warrior's build. Will you fight for this burh?'

'I will,' Alcuin said, although his breath caught in his chest at the idea of facing vikings. 'And Niclas, who's on his way, will do the same.'

'Good, I'll provide you with a shield and a spear each. I'll get the other men together.' Hasculf turned to the man standing at the gate and said, 'What are you waiting for, Odo? Call everybody out.'

The instruction was unnecessary. The commotion of his arrival had roused the burh and people emerged from their homes to stare at him. All the same, the man called Odo blew a call to arms on a horn.

That brought yet more men out, pulling on armour and lugging weapons and shields as they ran towards the gate. Women and children ran after them. Some helped with the weapons and armour as well as giving last-minute instructions to be careful and come back safely. One young man was given a particularly amorous kiss. Alcuin respectfully looked away.

At this moment Niclas arrived, huffing and puffing and red-faced. He was less than happy when Alcuin handed him a shield and spear.

'Really?' he muttered.

'Will you just cower behind the burh's wall then? When we have half a chance of getting Galen back?' Alcuin snapped.

He was ashamed to admit, even to himself, that he would like to do the same. Only his dread over what might happen to Galen acted as the spur that drove him to his foolish bravery. Niclas gave a sigh but took the weapon.

'What happened to Swidhelm?' Alcuin asked.

'I didn't hang about to find out,' Niclas said as he slipped his arm through the loops at the back of the circular shield. 'He was behind me. He'd be safer going to ground. Why are the men of this burh heading out, by the way?'

Alcuin wondered about that too. He'd have thought the burh residents would prefer to wait behind their walls and mount a defence there. But the reeve was obviously worried about Albreda who, Alcuin guessed, was his daughter. Either way, he was unwilling to wait.

'The people of Tiwham might still be holding out. We have to go to their aid,' Hasculf said.

He rammed on an impressive helmet. It had a stylised embossed brass dragon on the front that looped down the metal peg that protected his nose. He seemed to have his people's trust because the men fell in behind him without argument or even looking reluctant.

Alcuin took up the rear of the band of about forty men since he was less well provisioned and not a trained fighter. He guessed the only benefit of having him along was that he made their group look bigger. Strength in numbers was always worth having, or so his father had always said.

Alcuin glanced back at the burh as they marched away in time to see the gates being pushed shut. It sent a tremor of terror through him. This would be his first battle, and he was trying hard to be brave, but there was a sick feeling in the pit of his stomach.

Alcuin started praying. They were the most heartfelt prayers he'd ever made in his life. He alternated between begging God to protect him and begging Him to ensure that Galen survived.

They marched at high speed. The men were grim and silent, clutching their shields and their mixture of spears, swords and axes. They expected to see the viking raiders at any moment. But all the same, the walk back along the road seemed interminable. If it weren't for the smoke rising into the still air ahead of them, Alcuin might have expected Hasculf and his men to accuse him of lying.

That thought was put to rest as they heard an answering tramp of feet. Moments later, a band of vikings emerged from a copse. The two groups stopped for a moment, weighing each other up. Alcuin was so far back he couldn't see the vikings' faces, but he hoped they were surprised.

'Please, dear God and all the saints and angels, protect us all,' Alcuin whispered.

There was a roar from both sides. A viking warrior ran forward and hurled his spear at them. One of the young men leapt out of the shield wall ahead of Alcuin and threw his spear back at the viking. He got the viking in the arm,

whilst the other's weapon clattered against his shield and
the shaft split in two.

And so the battle commenced. An exchange of spears
continued. At the same time, men ran forward into a duel.
They grabbed their opponent's weapons and shield if they
got the better of him and rushed back to their own ranks.

For Alcuin, the battle dragged. It was like being trapped in
a horrific never-ending play. Weapons flashed about him.
Men shrieked and roared and blood flowed, lending its
scent to the stench of iron and sweat.

The vikings were warriors who did this for a living,
and their spears seemed to find their mark more often.
The townsfolk were reducing in number faster than the
vikings, although they still outnumbered the marauders.

That must have decided Hasculf to push harder because
he roared, 'Get them!' as he a set up a chant of, 'Out! Out!'

His men took up the cry as they pushed their shield wall
towards the tightly maintained wall of the vikings. Alcuin
pushed and shoved from the back, working with the rest
of the men to force the vikings further and further up the
road. For one astonishing moment, Alcuin saw the cart.
He hadn't realised how far they'd come.

But the fighting continued, both groups of men
pushing and jabbing, trying for the upper hand. Slowly,
inch by inch, they reached a burning hamlet. Here, the
pungent scent of smoke was added to the other smells of
battle.

The man in front of Alcuin took a solid blow to his leg that felled him. A viking warrior, roaring and covered in blood, now stood before Alcuin. He raised his shield on reflex and the man's axe slammed into it, screeching off the iron boss.

'Hang on!' Niclas shouted as he rammed his spear at the viking.

The tip sank into the man's arm. Alcuin, now in full panic, slammed the viking with his shield. He pushed him back and off his feet as Niclas stabbed him once again. This time he struck the viking's neck and it spurted blood.

Alcuin smashed him over his head with the shield. He was sick to his stomach with the man's death cries that were so loud they caused pain. Then they abruptly stopped as he died.

Hasculf shouted, 'Come on men, hurl them back into the river!'

With a roar, they gathered their strength and gave a mighty heave.

It was the critical moment. They pushed through the vikings, splitting them into two groups and causing chaos in their ranks. Now it was clear the vikings were losing. They fell back, regrouping, but the mood had changed. They wanted out. The risks were no longer worth the meagre bounty they'd made.

They didn't run, but they gave ground fast now and allowed themselves to be swept down to the river beach and into the water. Hasculf's men didn't wade after them. They stood jeering on the shore, banging their shields and watching as the vikings clambered back onto their boat and rowed away.

Alcuin couldn't believe they'd made it. As he watched
the ship, he became aware of his own rasping breath and
intense nausea seized him. He collapsed to his knees and
retched. His stomach was empty, but it made no difference
as he doubled over.

'Alright, enough,' Hasculf said as he gripped Alcuin
hard by the shoulder. 'I take it that was your first battle.'

Alcuin turned to face him and wiped his arm across his
tear-filled eyes and then his mouth, as he gave a weak nod.

'You did well. You have nothing to be ashamed of,'
Hasculf said, and turned to face the hamlet. 'Now let's see
if there are any survivors.'

He didn't look like he was expecting any, and Alcuin
doubted it too. The vikings had set the half dozen small
houses of the hamlet on fire and they were still burning,
or at least smouldering. Some bodies were visible, lying
splayed out in grotesque shapes, with pools of blood
around them, but there weren't many. The vikings had
taken the rest, along with their livestock. The people
would become thralls and most likely be sold in the slave
markets of Dublin.

'You, monk,' Hasculf said. 'Can you perform the last
rites?'

'I can.'

'Then you'd better come with me,' Hasculf said as he
headed for the first body.

It was a man, and clearly beyond help. It was also
obvious to Alcuin that Hasculf was not interested in most
of the bodies. He was moving quickly from one to the
next. They were mostly men and boys who must have died
while trying to fight the vikings. Whatever weapons they
had used were gone, though, taken by the pillagers.

Alcuin held his small wooden cross out over each
body they came to and murmured the prayer for
the dead before following Hasculf on his increasingly
desperate search. Alcuin found his own dread
mounting. He half expected to see Galen's black-robed
body, dragged to the hamlet and then abandoned. He
held his breath as they approached each hut and pushed
the door open.

'Oh God... Albreda,' Hasculf muttered as he spotted
the body of a girl lying on the ground. His face lost all
colour as he ran to the child and turned her over. 'No,
not Albreda, but where is she?'

Alcuin didn't say what he and everyone else who had
fanned out across the hamlet thought: the raiders had
taken the girl. Alcuin wondered whether Galen might
have been taken too. An icy fist of fear wrapped about
him that nearly left him bereft him of breath.

'You said there were two ships, didn't you?' Hasculf
said.

'I saw two ships, yes.'

Alcuin was grateful that he was being spoken to and
drawn back from his own terrifying thoughts.

'But when we got here, there was only one ship,'
Hasculf said.

'The other must have loaded up all they could carry
and left.'

'Aye, leaving their poorer brothers to march further
afield for their bounty.'

'So it seems.'

'And the cart we passed on the way? That was yours?'

'It was.'

'I didn't see any other monk.'

'No, that worries me too. But Brother Galen may have hidden, so... I am still hopeful I can track him down.'

'Why didn't he come with you?' Hasculf said as he kicked in the door of a smouldering house in a shower of sparks. The entry of fresh air made flames leap up, but Hasculf didn't notice and shouted into the swirling smoke, 'Albreda? Albreda, are you here?'

'There's nobody here,' Alcuin said, holding his arm up to his mouth and nose to protect himself from the acrid fumes. 'They have emptied this hamlet of all its people.'

'No Albreda and no sign of her aunt, either. It is bitter for me to see it is so,' Hasculf said. 'Now answer my question.'

'Brother Galen is very frail. He can't ride, and he threatened to kill himself to make me go away and leave him. He knew he'd slow us down.'

'Would he have killed himself?' Hasculf said, looking vaguely interested by this tale.

'I had no doubt he would do it. While I could have wrested the knife from his hand, I also knew I couldn't take him. We both did.'

'Odd,' Hasculf muttered. He turned around and surveyed the wrecked hamlet one more time. 'These vikings are a damned nuisance and no matter how much king Aethelred pays them, they will not go away.'

Alcuin shrugged. It wasn't his place to criticise the king.

Hasculf looked him over and said, 'You're nobility, aren't you?'

'I'm a monk now, so I've forsworn rank and wealth.'

'Once a noble, always a noble.'

Alcuin nodded acceptance. Now wasn't the time for a discussion on rank, anyway.

'Were the people of this hamlet under your protection?'

'Aye, and that's what's puzzling me. This isn't our first viking raid, so we're ready for them. All the hams around here are connected to one burh or another. They all have people on watch. The moment trouble rears its head, everyone either runs for the burh or vanishes into the marshes.'

'And that's effective, is it?' Alcuin asked, looking out over a vast expanse of reeds that surrounded the hamlet.

'You have to have grown up around here to not get lost or find yourself sucked down into the marsh and drowned.'

'I didn't realise it was that dangerous.'

'You're not from these parts, then. Any local knows not to wander off alone. So this is strange,' Hasculf said, pointing at the bodies. 'This hamlet shouldn't have been caught off guard.'

Alcuin had no idea what he should say in reply, but guessed he wasn't expected to have an answer anyway. Besides, worrying as that was, he was more concerned about Galen right now.

Hasculf sighed and gave the smouldering houses a final, sorrowful look. 'Well, come on, let's see if we can track down your fellow monk. Where did you leave him?'

'A little way from the cart.'

Alcuin was surprised by Hasculf's abrupt manner, but assumed he was working hard to hide his devastation at losing his daughter.

Hasculf gave orders for a handful of men to stay at the hamlet and see to the dead. The vikings had been thorough. It needed very few of them to bury the bodies and take away what was left and of use. Another group was already helping their fellow wounded fighters staunch bleeding and bind wounds. The worst of them were being carried back down the path that led to the burh.

CHAPTER 5

They toiled in silence back to the cart, picking up a few more injured men as they went. Alcuin hurried ahead. The dread of what he might find sat like a lump in his throat. He ran up to the cart and then stopped, staring at it in dismay. The vellum and inks were trampled into the dirt, but he didn't care about that at the moment.

He hoisted himself onto the vehicle, which was now open to the sky, and prayed he might find Galen. That was a futile hope. But he sighed with relief that his medical supplies were still there, tucked under the seat. He'd need those for Galen, if they ever found him. If not for him, then it could be used to help the men of the burh.

It seemed the vikings had only given the cart a cursory once over. They'd probably intended to come back and pillage it properly after they'd sacked Hasculf's burh. Well, that would not happen now.

Alcuin straightened up and, from his higher vantage point, looked around. There was no sign of Galen.

He took a deep breath and bellowed at the top of his lungs, 'Galen! Galen, where are you?'

A little girl sat up from amongst the pile of logs, saw Hasculf and shrieked, 'Father, Father, you've found me!' as she shot out into the road and into Hasculf's open arms.

'Albreda… Albreda, thank God!'

Hasculf swept the girl up into a savage embrace and covered her with kisses.

'Oh Father, I thought you'd never come,' the little girl sobbed. 'The vikings arrived at dawn, and Auntie bundled me up and ran with me through the smoke and the fighting to the edge of the hamlet. Then she pushed me out into the road and told me to run for help. But the vikings were too fast, and I fell and then this monk rescued me.'

'A monk?' Alcuin said, suddenly alert. 'Where? Where is he?'

'Over there, in the logs,' Albreda said, pointing to where she'd come from. 'He healed my knee, too. It's better now.'

'Yes?'

Hasculf was only paying half a mind to his child's words. With Albreda sitting high on his hip, he followed Alcuin's frantic dash to the logs.

At first, all Alcuin saw were shadows and churned up soil. Then he realised that what he'd mistaken for black, marshland mud, was actually a mud-covered black robe.

'Galen!' Alcuin reached for the hood and pushed it back with trembling, thick and useless fingers. 'Galen!' Alcuin said as he revealed a face as pale as wax.

'Is he still alive?' Hasculf asked.

It was a fair question. Galen was as still and cold as the bodies they'd found in the hamlet.

'Please God, let him be alive.'

Alcuin pressed his fingertips against Galen's throat, searching for a pulse, held his breath and prayed. There was a flutter, barely anything. He was so desperate he feared he was imagining it, and then there was another slight tremor.

'He's alive!' Relief made Alcuin feel weak, even more so than after the battle. 'But we must get him out of here.'

'Lift him onto the cart,' Hasculf said, gesturing for two of his men to help.

They hurried to the gap where one took a firm grasp of Galen's feet. The other, straddling over the logs, pulled Galen out by his arms.

'Careful,' Alcuin said, hurrying alongside. 'Don't hurt him.'

'We've got him,' Odo muttered as they carried Galen the short distance to the cart.

Niclas pulled away the backboard, and the men laid Galen on the floor. But as they carried out this operation, they made a shocking discovery.

'Ye Gods, blood,' Niclas said. 'Lots of it.'

'What is this?' Hasculf asked.

Alcuin felt as if he'd received a double blow. It was what he'd feared. But he didn't like to have his suspicions revealed in so graphic and public a way. What made it worse was that it looked like Galen had lost an awful lot of blood, which explained his extreme pallor.

The surrounding men were waiting for an explanation that Alcuin didn't want to give. If Galen survived, he'd not like all these strangers knowing what had happened to him. He didn't see what he could say, though.

To his surprise, Hasculf came to the rescue as he said, 'Looks like the vikings got to him before we did.'

'It would be just like those heathens to sodomise an innocent little monk,' the blond Odo said with a dark scowl.

Niclas looked up in surprise, but Alcuin directed a quelling glare at him and he shut his mouth with a snap. This was the least of his problems, anyway.

'Could we go, please?' Alcuin said. 'I need to get Brother Galen to safety. I also need to do what I can to stem the bleeding and get him out of these wet robes and warmed up.'

'Of course,' Hasculf said. 'It isn't safe to be out here, anyway. You stay with your friend in the cart. See what you can do straight away. We'll get you back to Wodenshurst as quickly as possible.'

'Thank you,' Alcuin said as he hopped into the cart.

Hasculf gave an accepting nod, hoisted his daughter higher on his hip and set off with a long, easy stride. His men grabbed the shaft of the cart, dragged it out of the ruts and set off at a slower pace.

Alcuin pulled Galen into his arms and held him tight to make sure he wasn't thrown about and to get him warm. He also prayed to God and every saint he could think of to save his friend. He'd never seen Galen in such a dangerous state, and he feared the worst.

He blamed himself for forcing Galen onto the mule. There was no doubt the brief ride and the fall had caused Galen's old injury to bleed so grievously. Galen must have been in agony. He must have thought there was no hope for him. That was why he'd been so willing to force Alcuin to leave.

'Please, God, please,' Alcuin muttered for the hundredth time. 'Please save him.'

The women of the burh were already seeing to the walking wounded by the time Hasculf and Alcuin arrived with the cart bearing Galen. They pulled into a narrow square just inside the entrance to the palisade. The sturdy wooden gates were pulled shut behind them. Then they were barred with a log the width of a sizeable tree that required two men to hoist into position.

The square itself was filled with warriors, some treating their own wounds, some supporting their fellows. One man had his hand clamped down on the gushing leg wound of his friend who was keening in pain. He wasn't the only one, but he was the worst and he'd attracted the attention of two women who were running to help him.

A tall, slim woman, with her mousy brown hair tied back in a long plait, looked to be in charge. She was shouting instructions over the noise to get the women to those she thought looked most in need of help.

The moment she spotted Hasculf and the girl, she shrieked, 'Albreda!' and ran over to her beaming husband.

She took the child's hand, squeezing it, and caressed her smiling face.

'Yes, she's safe, my wife,' Hasculf said.

'My sister?' Ivetta murmured.

Hasculf shook his head, and his face wrinkled with regret.

'Now we need your help to see to the man who rescued our daughter.'

'Yes, of course, anything for such a man!'

Ivetta banished her sorrow. There would be time to grieve later.

'He's in the cart.'

Hasculf quickly filled in his wife on what had happened to Galen and why he'd been left behind. Ivetta listened intently as she went to the cart and examined the unconscious Galen cradled in Alcuin's arms. She first touched his forehead with the back of her hand. Then she checked whether he was breathing by holding a small bronze disk up to his mouth. It misted up, but only a little.

'I'll leave Brother Alcuin to help you,' Hasculf said and turned his attention back to his men. 'Man the battlements! And all who are fit, or have already had your wounds seen to, stand ready. We've not seen the last of those damned vikings.'

His words chilled Alcuin, but he had a more immediate concern.

Ivetta tilted her head, considering him for a moment before she said, 'Your friend is gravely injured. We have to work quickly.'

'Are you a healer?' Alcuin asked.

Ivetta seemed to know what she was doing and Alcuin liked her decided air, but he felt he should make doubly certain.

'I have some skill in that area,' Ivetta said. 'And I'm afraid I'm the best you have in this burh. Considering how ill your Brother Galen is, I doubt he'd last long if you tried to take him to the next burh.'

'I wouldn't dream of moving him, especially not when the vikings might return. I will follow your instructions.'

Ivetta gave a quick business-like nod, apparently pleased not to have to argue with anyone when she had work to do.

'Cyneburg, Aelbfled,' she shouted, and a well-built, red-haired woman and a much smaller and slimmer brunette hurried to her side. 'Let's get Brother Galen into the old reeve's hut.'

'Randwind's house?' Cyneburg said. 'Is that a good idea?'

'There's no time to argue,' Ivetta said.

With the help of the women, Alcuin hoisted Galen onto his back. He noted the blood that had spread across the cart floor. It spurred him into greater action. With Cyneburg keeping a firm hand on Galen's back, Alcuin half ran and half staggered after Ivetta.

She made her way down a narrow lane made dark by the closeness of the houses. Ivetta stopped at the largest house in another little square, which was more like a widening in the road, and threw open the door.

Aelbfled hurried inside and straight to a narrow bed that was set against one wall. She pulled the sheepskins away and pounded them, raising a cloud of dust. Alcuin got the impression the house wasn't currently in use. It was filled with cobwebs, there was a hole in the thatch above and, aside from the bed, it appeared everything else had been taken away. More worryingly, it had a cross, meant to ward off evil, carved into the doorpost.

'Quickly, we have to get this wet habit off him,' Ivetta said, breaking into Alcuin's thoughts.

'Of course,' Alcuin said as he lowered Galen onto the bed.

The women closed about Galen, and Alcuin could do nothing but stand back and resume praying. Ivetta pulled at the knotted rope belt around Galen's waist. Then, working from the hem upwards, the women rolled the robe up and over Galen's head in one practised move.

Alcuin had never seen Galen without his clothes. He was shocked to discover that the robes made him look bigger than he actually was. Lying naked on the bed, Alcuin could make out every rib and every knobbly bone of his spine. Then his gaze swept down to Galen's thighs, and he had to suppress the nausea that rolled up to see them covered in thick, clotted blood.

'No, Aelbfled, don't waste time trying to get him clean,' Ivetta said as she rolled Galen onto his side. It was the position Alcuin had always seen him in when he was in Brother Benesing's house. 'We have to get him warm first. We'll worry about the bleeding later.'

'I have medicines,' Alcuin said, recalled to his duties, and he held out the bag given to him by Brother Benesing.

'We'll look at that later, too. We can't get any medicines into him out cold as he is.'

Ivetta flung a thick woollen blanket over Galen and ordered Cyneburg to light a fire in the hearth. It was a shallow pit in the centre of the room. Cyneburg got it going and up to a good blaze in a matter of minutes. The smoke rose straight up and then vanished as it drifted through the thatch.

Alcuin hung back, helpless and out of place. He also felt deeply guilty that he'd left his friend behind. But he knew better than to get in Ivetta's way. She was doing all that was possible for Galen, and he had to be patient.

After the initial flurry of activity, Ivetta said, 'I can do the rest unaided. You two go back to treating our men.'

'Thank you,' Cyneburg said, and she and Aelbfled hurried away.

Their husbands, brothers or sons were probably amongst the wounded. It added another layer to Alcuin's

guilt that they had dropped everything to help Galen.
Then again, he was also the most severely injured.

Ivetta unfolded a little three-legged stool with a
strap-like leather seat, placed it beside Galen, and sat
down with a sigh. She leaned closer and inspected
his face. Then she reached under the sheepskin, drew
out his arm, pulled off the glove on his left hand and
examined his scarred palm. Finally, she looked up at
Alcuin, still standing at the edge of the room.

'You'd better tell me the truth.'

'What?' Alcuin said, mortified that Ivetta had found
him out so easily in a lie.

'My husband thinks the vikings raped your young
monk, but it seems that he's been carrying an injury for
a long time. One which causes him considerable pain,'
Ivetta said, twisting Galen's palm to the light of the
open door. 'If I am to give him the proper treatment,
I need to know what that injury is.'

'Will you keep what I have to say in confidence?'

'Of course. It is nobody else's business, after all.'

'Well...' Alcuin said, gathering his courage. 'Galen
was raped, but it wasn't by the vikings. It was quite a
few years ago, and it caused permanent damage.'

'So that he bleeds from his old injury?'

'I treated him too roughly when we were trying to get
away from the vikings and I fear it's my fault he started
to bleed.'

'Well, we must stop the bleeding now, before it's too
late.'

'I was given instructions on how to treat him,' Alcuin
said, pulling out Benesing's letter.

'You will have to read it to me,' Ivetta said, 'for that I cannot do. And before you start, show me the medicines you have.'

Alcuin was happy to comply. He'd never dreamed he'd have to treat Galen for a serious injury. He'd just expected to watch over him and make sure he didn't receive one.

Ivetta, thankfully, seemed to know what she was doing. She listened to what Alcuin was reading while she went through his bundle of herbs and syrups. Then she decanted a thick syrup that smelled of honey and coated her index finger with it. She lifted the blanket and reached towards Galen's bottom. Alcuin hastily averted his gaze.

'What are you doing?' he asked in horror.

'Stopping the bleeding.'

'But Brother Benesing didn't say to do it that way,' Alcuin said, flapping his hand vaguely as he turned away.

'No, but from what you have read, he didn't expect the injury to be so bad again, either. But the herb and the honey in this syrup is good at stopping wounds from bleeding, so we will try it in this way. And believe me, Brother Alcuin, I wouldn't be doing this if I didn't believe the case to be desperate.'

'Right,' Alcuin said, still very shaken.

'You keep reading. That Brother Benesing has much sense in what he says.'

'So you understand it?' Alcuin said with a modicum of relief.

'Not all of it, but enough.'

'That's more than I can say.'

Alcuin went back to reading the letter aloud whilst Ivetta began wiping the blood off Galen's legs and back. She used a cloth that she dipped into a bowl of water and rinsed out now and then, turning the water deep red in the process.

While she worked, she muttered an incantation under her breath. Alcuin was familiar enough with that behaviour. Most people he knew who practised the healing arts used incantations. They helped protect the afflicted from the elves who brought down illness.

The only healer he'd ever seen go about his work silently was Brother Benesing. He was Galen's uncle and the infirmarius at the Abbey of Yarmwick. Alcuin wondered why he didn't use the incantations. Maybe he did, but he didn't speak them out loud.

Once she apparently decided she could do no more, Ivetta covered Galen with the blanket again. She then returned to her position by the head of the bed and examined his face.

'It looks like it was a very violent attack. How old was he at the time?'

'Around thirteen,' Alcuin said.

'And now?'

'He's sixteen, two years younger than me.'

'So he has carried this injury for three years?'

'It hasn't been easy for him.'

'No indeed. But he is a valued member of your community, is he?'

'He's very shy, but he's alright.'

'I think there's more to the tale,' Ivetta said, 'but I won't press you. I'll only ask for the information I need to heal him.'

Alcuin was thankful for that. As a healer and a mother, Ivetta would disapprove of the way Galen had been treated in the monastery for his first couple of years there. Further discussion on any topic ended with Albreda's arrival. She was still in her muddy dress, but looking none the worse for her ordeal.

'Mama, may I come in?' the little girl whispered.

'Of course, my darling,' Ivetta said, and her face softened at the joy of seeing her daughter.

'It's boiling in here,' Albreda said as she ran to her mother and gave her a tight hug.

Alcuin watched the pair. The girl had a very similar face to her mother, with a thin straight nose and generous lips. But she was darker, with chestnut brown hair that more closely resembled her father's.

'We have to keep it warm for Brother Galen.'

Albreda nodded as she looked down at Galen's pale face. 'He fixed my knee, Mama.'

'Did he, my dear? How did he do that?'

'I don't know,' Albreda said with an expansive shrug, 'but it doesn't hurt anymore and I can walk properly now.'

'Really?' Ivetta said as she pushed up her daughter's dress and examined her knee. 'Holy Mary, Mother of God!' she breathed in surprise.

'What is it?' Alcuin asked, astonished at Ivetta's reaction.

All he could see were two ordinary, somewhat muddy, knees.

'My daughter was born with a deformed right knee. No matter what remedies I tried, it remained swollen, stiff and painful. Now it looks perfect.'

'It was the monk,' Albreda said.

Ivetta looked doubtfully at Galen.

Then she turned earnest, searching eyes on Alcuin and asked, 'Is he a saint?'

'Galen?!' Alcuin said with a bark of surprised laughter. 'No, of course not.'

'But my daughter says he healed her, and her knee is most certainly no longer deformed.'

'Galen can't even heal himself. How could he have healed your daughter?' Alcuin said, alarmed by this turn of events.

'I don't know,' Ivetta said. 'I know nothing about miracles.'

CHAPTER 6

Alcuin laid his cape at the foot of the bed and snatched a couple of hours of rest between watching over Galen. Sleep was hard to come by. He'd been shocked to find himself in the middle of a battle. Now, whenever he closed his eyes, images of screaming men and flashing weapons and the smell of sweat and blood invaded his mind.

The worst was the memory of the man he'd had a hand in killing. He would only just drop off when he'd be pulled, sobbing, back to wakefulness, the man's death cries still ringing in his ears.

So for himself and for Galen, he spent most of his time on his knees, his elbows resting on the edge of Galen's bed, praying. It was the only thing he could do to distract himself and help his friend. Galen remained as pale as parchment and motionless.

Alcuin constantly checked that he was still breathing. He'd place his hand on Galen's chest and wait, in dread-filled silence, to see whether it would rise. It was always a profound relief when it did. Alcuin feared that the next time he looked, it wouldn't.

Thankfully, Ivetta came by regularly to see how Galen was doing. On her first visit, she arrived with an armful of charms. She placed one at the foot of the bed. She put another one under the cushions that had been taken from the cart and were now being used as pillows. She stuck another two on either side of the hearth and one over the door.

Most were tracts of text written on parchment so ancient that it had turned a deep brown. Since Ivetta couldn't read, Alcuin guessed that the charms had been handed down to her by past healers. Alcuin was familiar with some charms because he'd grown up with similar things in his father's hall.

All the same, he said, 'What's that for?'

'Your letter said that Brother Galen takes a fever when he bleeds.' Ivetta stood on a stool and hung a posy of dried herbs off the hook screwed into the beam that ran over the bed. 'These are charms to keep the elves away so they don't bring a fever down upon Brother Galen.'

Alcuin nodded acceptance. That was another thing Brother Benesing never did: he never mentioned elves in relation to sickness. But Alcuin knew that the common people believed in these magical beings interfering with their lives. If he was scrupulously honest, he had to admit that he still hung on to the suspicion that they existed too.

Then Ivetta put out the fire.

'Really?' Alcuin said. 'Doesn't he need it any longer?'

'I think not. Brother Galen has warmed up a bit and stopped bleeding. These are both positive signs.'

'I am relieved you say that. I thought there was no improvement.'

'We are still at a dangerous moment. You must remain vigilant.'

'I will.'

Alcuin had no intention of stopping his vigil, but he was glad the fire was no longer needed. The heat had been oppressive and sent rivulets of sweat trickling down his back.

Ivetta had just left and Alcuin resumed his praying when he realised that someone else had arrived.

'How is he doing?' Hasculf asked as he stepped into the hut, swinging a large sack.

Alcuin jumped to his feet and said, 'He's still with us. But I fear if he doesn't wake soon and get some fluids into him, he won't make it.'

'I'm sorry to hear that,' Hasculf murmured. 'I brought you this, by the way.'

Alcuin took the sack and peered inside. At first, he wondered why he was being given a load of what appeared to be mud-soaked leaves and lumpy stones.

'My men went back to the clearing where we found Brother Galen,' Hasculf said in response to Alcuin's raised eyebrows. 'They gathered that lot up from the road. I thought you might be able to salvage something from it.'

'Our supplies.' Alcuin realised the leaves were actually crumpled sheets of vellum and the lumps were their pots of ink. 'Thank you.'

'It might also keep you occupied. It's better to have something to work on.'

'What of the vikings?' Alcuin asked with more trepidation than he hoped he showed.

'We're still keeping the burh shut and we're waiting. I've sent a couple of my men out to scout and a couple more to the neighbouring burhs to see if the vikings attacked them. Now it's a waiting game.'

'I will pray we come through safely.'

'That would be good,' Hasculf said with a nod as he strolled away.

Alcuin tipped the contents of the sack onto the floor and took stock. A mindless task like cleaning the mud off the sheets of vellum was what he needed. And he could do it here, where he could also keep an eye on Galen.

There were a good few bundles of the eight-page gatherings that would be alright once he cleaned them. Thankfully, most of the inks had also survived being trampled, although he'd lost all his green ink. Their precious gold leaf was also gone.

Alcuin started organising the contents of the sack into little piles. He put the vellum on his left, paints in the middle, and the large pile of pens and brushes to his right. Then he fetched the bucket of water and cloth that had been left when the women had cleaned Galen. He'd started with wiping the pens down when Niclas appeared. He stood in the doorway and cleared his throat while staring fixedly at his toes.

'How... how is Brother Galen?'

'It's too early to say,' Alcuin said, looking the man up and down.

He was right to feel ashamed. He'd abandoned Alcuin and Galen in his rush to escape the vikings, although he had come some way to redeeming himself by saving Alcuin in the battle. Niclas now looked at a loss, drawing aimlessly on the ground with the tip of one worn boot.

'You can help me clean this lot,' Alcuin said.

Niclas gave a deep relieved sigh, squatted in the doorway and reached for a pen.

'You can actually come inside,' Alcuin said.

Niclas shook his head.

'I'll wait till Brother Galen has recovered. Until then, I'll keep watch from outside.'

'Suit yourself,' Alcuin said, and went back to his own cleaning efforts.

There was something soothing about sharing a task. Words became superfluous as it was the companionship that mattered. Alcuin glanced back at Galen lying still in the bed. He would prefer to do this with Galen, but Niclas would suffice for now.

While they worked, Alcuin took his first proper look at his surroundings. He'd already realised that Hasculf's burh was a small place. It was surrounded by marshland, so the burh itself had less land upon which to put up houses. That explained why all the buildings were closer together than at his and Galen's home. It was also overseen by a shire reeve, Hasculf, rather than an ealdorman. That was another indicator of its lesser importance.

The burh, though, was alive with sights, sounds and smells. Many of the smells were provided by the livestock. They were all gathered in from the fields to keep them safe from raiders. Every burh had a fair collection of livestock within its walls, most penned near the homes of their owners. But only a town expecting an attack brought so much of its livestock inside.

There were pigs, goats, sheep and chickens wandering the streets, gobbling up anything that fell to the ground. There was even a pair of cows tethered to a nearby house, one of which was currently being milked. Their moos, bleats and clucks filled the air, and their dung added a pungent layer of smells.

A chatting, laughing group of women were washing clothes in a large trough set at the furthest end of the

narrow square. Alcuin wondered whether they were
doing their laundry inside for fear of the vikings.
He assumed they'd usually have used the river. Other
women must be preparing food, because he could smell
baking bread and the musty aroma of brewing beer.

Alcuin guessed that, despite the risks, some men
were either fishing or in the fields getting the last of
their crops in. The greater number, though, were on
the lookout for viking raiders. Aside from the men he
couldn't see, there were some craftsmen hard at work
in the houses along the square.

There was a cobbler opposite, seated in front of his
house under the shade of the overhanging thatched
roof, sewing shoes. A couple of cowhides dried in the
sun beside him, stretched tight over frames. They added
a familiar and not too pleasant tanner's stench to the
air.

A potter was hard at work, rolling out a coil of clay
at the house next door. He would then shape it into a
pot or drinking vessel and pinch the clay together till it
was watertight.

A sudden banging of metal against metal started
up. Alcuin leaned around the doorway of the hut to
discover a blacksmith. He was stripped to his waist and
banging away at a glowing metal rod. Going by the size
and shape, it looked like he was making spearheads in
anticipation of the vikings' return.

Alcuin wished he could pretend that all of this looked
like the normal, everyday life of a well-tended burh. But
having so many packed inside in the middle of the day
wasn't normal, and he could sense the underlying tension
in the people. They were all working with an attentive air,

listening for the alarm that would signal the next viking attack.

'Will you still be able to make a book for the king with this?' Niclas asked, holding up a battered and mud-stained gathering of vellum pages.

Alcuin sighed and scratched his head.

'I don't know. I'll have to clean everything, then sand it with a pumice stone and finally buff it with chalk. Then I'll know if the pages are pristine enough to be made into the king's book. If not, they'll still be useable for a lesser document.'

'But what about the king's book, then? Will he have supplies you can use?'

'If not him, then there is sure to be a supplier of vellum and inks we can approach in Lundenburh. The king already paid for everything, though, so there will have to be some renegotiation. Thankfully, I won't have to do that. That will be for the king and our abbot to resolve.'

'Is a book like the one for the king expensive?' Niclas asked as he brushed off the dark dried mud.

'Very. The king isn't only paying for the items needed to create such a codex. He's also paying for my time and Galen's and for our abilities.'

'Is he likely to reward you and Brother Galen for all that work?'

'He'll reward the abbey. We monks aren't supposed to accumulate riches.'

'But the abbey can?'

'Only if the money is used to succour the poor or to the glory of God. And also because we need money to buy spices and cloth and some other items that we can't produce ourselves.'

'It's not a bad life being a monk though, is it?'

'It has its moments,' Alcuin said as he pulled a paintbrush through the cloth to get it clean.

'Better than being a thrall.'

'I'd say anything is better than that.'

'Aye, you're not far wrong.'

Something in the tone of his voice made Alcuin ask, 'Do you know about that, Niclas?'

'I was born a thrall,' Niclas said.

'Ah!'

Alcuin was getting more information about Niclas than he wanted. But it seemed the man was in a talkative mood, and Alcuin could also use the distraction.

'When I reached adulthood,' Niclas said, 'my fellow thralls and I were set free when my master died. We could have remained with the master's wife, but she no longer had a use for us. She went off to live with her brother and he didn't want all the extra mouths.'

'He could have sold you all.'

'He wanted to, but the old mistress was a good woman and she spoke to the ealdorman. He supported her request over her brother's greed and gave us our freedom. Not that all of us wanted it, mind you.

'I did. I was young and strong. I figured I could make something of myself. The older ones, though, they weren't so sure. I wouldn't be surprised if some of them didn't lay their heads back into the hands of somebody powerful.'

'That is often the way.'

'Not for me,' Niclas said, putting a bit more vigour into the cleaning. 'I'll never go back into thraldom. I might change professions one day, though. I might even become a monk.'

'Really?'

'Maybe one day, when I'm old.'

'You'll have to be very old,' Alcuin said, laughing at the idea, 'because, from everything I saw in Hugh's hall, you flirt with every pretty young thing.'

'Aye well, there's the problem,' Niclas said. 'I'm dick-led and no doubt about it. But if you'll not take it too unkindly in me, I couldn't help noticing that your eyes linger on the pretty girls, too.'

'That is my trial,' Alcuin sighed. 'Sometimes it takes all the self-discipline at my disposal to keep my hands and eyes off women. And it doesn't help that those same women flaunt themselves at me with scant regard for how difficult they are making my life.'

'I've noticed women often have an eye for the religious types,' Niclas said. 'Truly, they are the Devil's own handiwork, tempting us as they do. But you're a handsome fellow too, with your blond hair and blue eyes, so I don't suppose I can blame them. I do blame them for making sheep's eyes at Master Galen, though, when everyone can see he isn't the least bit interested.'

'I wouldn't be so sure of that,' Alcuin said, leaping immediately to Galen's defence.

'You mean he actually likes women?'

'Did you still think he was a catamite?'

Alcuin was aware that his former irritation with Niclas was coming out in his voice. Niclas picked up on it and gave him an apologetic smile.

'He often seems more like a woman than a man, the way he's so soft-spoken and all. It made me wonder. And, truth be told, I know it's a cardinal sin and all, but... if they leave me alone, I don't care what they do.'

This was turning into an altogether more astonishing conversation than Alcuin had expected. The carter sounded entirely sincere.

'Well, I can assure you that Galen is no sodomite. In fact, he has quite a crush on Cwengyth.'

Alcuin regretted his hasty words the moment he'd spoken them. It was no business of Niclas's and it would only embarrass Galen.

Niclas, though, didn't seem to think anything of that indiscretion as he heaved a great sigh.

'Now *there* is a magnificent creature. But I could be a piece of dung for all the attention she ever gives me.'

'Me too,' Alcuin said with a laugh, determined to move the subject away from Galen. 'Although I'd have been in serious trouble with that household if I'd tried to attract her attention. So I stayed well away.'

'Shame on you. Do you actually seduce women? And you a monk!'

'No, I don't, but I see nothing wrong with being friendly and chatting to them. I just try to keep it at that.'

Another day passed without Galen taking in any food or water. Ivetta looked more and more grave, so Alcuin prepared his heart for the worst. Heaven only knew what he'd do if Galen did die, though.

How would he tell Ealdorman Hugh that he'd left Galen to the mercy of the vikings? Would that rekindle the blood feud between his family and Galen's? Would they accuse him of deliberately leaving Galen behind? If Galen died, would he even care what others thought? The mere idea of losing Galen was unbearable.

The sound of a girl clearing her throat shook Alcuin from these dreadful thoughts. He opened his eyes, midway through his prayer, and looked the girl up and down. Today she was in a green dress. The straps over the shoulders fastened to the overdress with small, exquisitely wrought silver clasps. She was a child her parents doted upon. It gave her a confidence most seven-year-old girls lacked.

'Can I come in?' Albreda asked, even though she was already at the hearthside. 'I've brought you some food.'

Alcuin accepted the bowl of pottage she held out to him, a wooden spoon standing upright in the stew.

'Thank you.'

'Mother said you have to eat it even if you don't feel like eating. She said you have to keep your strength up, for she can't have two sick monks on her hands.'

Alcuin smiled at that. Clearly, the girl was giving him those instructions verbatim. He wondered whether Ivetta had hoped her daughter would be more diplomatic.

'I will eat it, don't worry.'

Alcuin settled on the little three-legged stool and scooped up a large mouthful of pottage. It looked good: a mixture of vegetables, dried peas and beans. To his surprise, Albreda sat down, cross-legged, on the floor and gazed up at him.

'Why are you in Randwind's house?' Albreda asked.

'Am I in Randwind's house?' Alcuin said.

'You are.'

'And who is Randwind?'

'He was the old reeve before my father,' Albreda said. 'He's dead now. He had no children, so he trained my father up to be the next reeve.'

'I see.'

Alcuin supposed it was useful information. This burh of Wodenshurst was unfamiliar territory. He wasn't used to spending so much time amongst strangers. It would unnerve Galen, too. It was good he was learning more about them so he could tell Galen when he woke.

'It's a very fine house. Why did nobody move into it after the reeve died?'

'Elves,' Albreda said, with an eloquent shudder. 'There are more elves in this house than in any other in the burh. Old Randwind ended up talking to them all the time. He was always muttering away in here, by himself, only talking to elves.'

Alcuin gave an understanding nod.

'I have heard tell that when a person is growing old, the elves gather about them, waiting.'

'Waiting for what?' Albreda said, examining Alcuin with her disconcertingly direct gaze.

'Waiting for them to die, so they can snatch up their souls.'

'But what happens then?' Albreda said, her hazel eyes widening in awe-filled anticipation.

'I don't know. Maybe a saint intervenes and gets the soul away from them and guides it to heaven.'

'Is that what your books say?'

'The books in the monastery never mention elves at all.'

'Oh,' Albreda said. 'Why not?'

'I don't know. Maybe because they don't have elves in the warm southern countries. That's where the pope lives and where most of the saints seem to come from.'

'But Brother Galen doesn't come from there,' Albreda said, looking up at his still white face.

'Brother Galen isn't a saint, Albreda. You mustn't say that he is.'

'But he fixed my knee.'

'How? Did he lay his hand on your knee?' Alcuin asked, because the issue had been bothering him. So much so that he'd spent much of his time mulling it over.

'No, he just grabbed me and held me tight and afterwards my knee was better.'

'Well,' Alcuin said, trying to think the thing through, 'I don't know how that happened, but it wasn't Galen.'

'Yes it was, and he–' Albreda stopped, her eyes wide and fixed on Galen's face.

Alcuin looked too and realised that he was awake.

'Galen, thank God!' Mindful of Ivetta's instructions, Alcuin grabbed the bowl of gruel with the spout that Ivetta had prepared for this moment. 'Albreda, I'll hold his head up. You get the gruel into his mouth.'

Alcuin shoved the bowl into the girl's hands. Then he lifted Galen by his shoulders and supported his head against his body. Galen barely reacted to this manhandling. He blinked vaguely at everyone and his eyes started to close.

'No, Galen! Stay awake!' Alcuin shouted. 'You must eat something.'

Galen lay slumped in Alcuin's arms, not even struggling, and choked on the gruel as Albreda tipped it into his mouth. But somehow he swallowed some. Alcuin had to be happy with that because, as he lowered him back onto the bed, Galen's eyes were already shut.

'Is that good? Is it good he woke up?' Albreda asked.

'I must suppose that it is. When your mother comes to visit this evening, I'll ask her what she thinks.'

'Well, I think it's a good sign,' Albreda said as she returned to her cross-legged position.

It wasn't Ivetta who first appeared at the house in the evening. Alcuin heard people approach and expected to see Ivetta and Albreda. Instead, he looked up into the faces of two strangers. They were a very young-looking man with a chubby face and fuzzy beard and an even younger and nervous fair-haired woman clutching a swaddled baby.

'Please, my lord,' the man said, giving a deep bow, 'we heard the monk in the bed is a saint who can heal deformities.'

'Well, he isn't, so you may as well go away,' Alcuin said in a less harsh tone than he might have used.

He was sympathetic to anyone who worried about their children, especially when the child looked as pinched and unhealthy as the wax-like little face in the bundle before him. But once rumours started, they were always so difficult to scotch. He wanted to stop this one before it got out of hand.

'The thing is,' the young woman said, 'our little boy was born sickly and with a club foot. We were hoping... well, we'd do anything if the saintly monk can heal him.'

'Are you people blind as well as foolish?' Alcuin said, being cruel to stop this rumour from getting out of control. 'Look at Galen. He's ill. He could be dying. How can you expect him to perform a miracle for you under these circumstances?'

'If he could only touch our boy,' the young man said. He obviously knew he was overstepping a boundary, but he was so desperate, he was going to do it anyway. And he'd make sure he got a miracle before the saint expired. 'We'd be very grateful.'

Alcuin wanted to throw them out with an order never to return. Then it occurred to him that if Galen was to touch the baby and not heal him, it might put an end to all this foolishness.

'Alright, bring the child here.'

'Thank you, my lord!'

The woman hurried to Galen's bedside and dropped to her knees before him. She held her baby out as if he were an offering. Alcuin drew Galen's thin, pale hand out from under the covers and placed it on the child's head.

The woman looked uncertainly up at him and then down at Galen's hand.

'Should something happen?'

'I doubt it.' Alcuin suddenly felt sorry for the girl. All she wanted was for her child to be normal and healthy. 'I hope for your sakes that something does come of this.'

'Thank you,' the woman said, already looking forlorn, as if her last hope had just fled. 'You understand we... we had to try.'

'Yes, I understand,' Alcuin said and watched the couple leave.

Their shoulders were slumped in dejected resignation. He sat down on the little stool beside Galen and mulled over the strange event. Galen's hand, still hanging out of the bed as Alcuin had left it, twitched.

'Galen?'

Galen's eyes flicked open, vague and out of focus.

'Alcuin? Alcuin, is that you?' he whispered.

'Yes, it's me. Thank God you recognise me.'

'Alcuin,' Galen said, his hand grasping anxiously on to his friend's arm, 'where are we?'

'We're safe, never fear, in a burh by the river.'

'You came back for me,' Galen said with a sigh.

'I did.'

Galen's words made Alcuin smart with shame that he'd left the man behind.

'What of the vikings?' Galen asked, and a note of anxiety returned to his voice.

'We chased them back onto their ships and they haven't returned. Hasculf is keeping the burh gates closed and has doubled the watch. He also has men stationed all along the river on the lookout for more ships to ensure they don't sneak back.' This brief talk had exhausted Galen, so Alcuin stopped and said, 'Wait, don't go to sleep until you've had something to eat. We have to get your strength up.'

Galen nodded and, fortunately, didn't resist this time when Alcuin put the spout of gruel in his mouth. He even managed to finish half its contents before his eyes drifted shut again. Try as he might, Alcuin couldn't rouse him.

'Leave him be,' Ivetta said from the doorway.

'He was awake. He had some more gruel. But now he's out cold again.'

'There is no reason to fret. It seems he's on the road to recovery.'

'Really?'

'Yes, Brother Alcuin. So you can wipe that look of anxiety, which has been your constant companion, from your face.'

'He didn't take a fever either.'

'The charms seem to have done their job then. But don't relax your guard yet. Elves can be tricky little beggars.'

CHAPTER 8

The raucous call of what sounded like an army of roosters woke Galen. He opened his eyes to a pale grey dawn and tried to locate at least one of the offending beasts that seemed to be right at his door. It was ajar, but he couldn't see what was happening outside. So with a sigh, Galen turned to gaze into the cobweb-filled depths of the roof and watched as several dusty strands swayed back and forth in the breeze.

On the beam overhead was a bundle of herbs he suspected was a charm. He wished it wasn't there. But he felt heavy and incapable of movement and not up to getting onto the bed to remove it.

He also couldn't work out where he was, nor where Alcuin had vanished off to, and that increased his anxiety. He looked back down and examined the floor. A low pallet stood close to his, a black cloak folded at the foot. That was surely where Alcuin was sleeping.

Galen had a feeling Alcuin had already told him most of the information he was wondering about. But it didn't seem to stick. Not only that, but he'd come to a horrible realisation, and he needed Alcuin's help to resolve it. Galen suppressed the flicker of fear that Alcuin was no longer around. He wouldn't leave him, not unless his hand was forced.

Galen closed his eyes and offered up a prayer of thanks to God for his rescue. He also asked God to continue to keep everyone safe. Galen decided against making the more trivial request that Alcuin come back quickly.

He half wished he could remember more clearly what had happened when the vikings had come. Then again, he was relieved that the memory was as insubstantial as a nightmare. He had more than enough harsh memories to deal with. He could live without one more.

'Galen?' Alcuin said.

Just hearing his voice relieved Galen of so many worries. Alcuin was laden down with a bowl of food and some kind of mug with a spout.

'Ah, you're looking much better this morning.' Alcuin beamed at him as if he'd achieved an impressive feat. 'Maybe you can even sit up today.'

'Alcuin!' Galen said, remembering his most urgent dilemma.

'Yes, it's me,' Alcuin said with an amused smile. 'Did you fear I'd abandoned you?'

'No, not that. Alcuin... I don't have any clothes on!'

Galen was deeply mortified to have to say anything about this. He also kept his fingers wrapped around the top of the blanket and pulled it up to his chin.

'Is that all that's worrying you?' Alcuin said with a sudden laugh. 'Thank God! Now I know you are on the mend for you to be fretting about such a trivial thing. We had to get your robes off to treat you and the women took them away to wash all the mud and the blood off.'

'Can I have them back, please?' Galen said, relieved that he had solved this mystery.

'Of course. I'll get Ivetta and one of her women to help dress you.'

'No! Not women,' Galen said, turning bright red with embarrassment. 'Please not, Alcuin.'

'Well, I can't do it by myself.'

'What happened to Niclas?' Galen asked, seized by another frightening thought.

'He's fine, no need to worry. He's in the burh somewhere. If I'm any judge, he's flirting with some local maiden. The man's incorrigible.'

'He could help dress me, couldn't he?'

'I suppose so. I don't know how gentle either of us will be, but if it's what you'd like, then we'll do it.'

Galen nodded and murmured, 'The sooner the better, please.'

'I will go now as long as you promise to eat everything I've brought.'

'I give you my word,' Galen said, glancing down at a thin pottage.

Today his stomach grumbled, and he had an edge of hunger that was rare for him. So it was no trial to eat while Alcuin went in search of Niclas and his clothes.

'Master Galen,' Niclas said as his frame blocked the light coming through the open doorway. 'Thank goodness you are looking better. I've been offering up prayers for your recovery every day in the church.'

'So you should,' Alcuin murmured and shook out the robes he had slung over his shoulder and placed them on the bed. 'Let's give this a go, then.'

Galen pushed his covers down to his waist and held out his arms, much as a child did when their mother dressed them. He was relieved not to be dressed by strangers. And so happy to get his habit back that he wasn't even embarrassed to be naked before Alcuin and Niclas.

The two men tried their best to get Galen into his tunic without hurting him and, mostly, were successful.

'Oh, Master Galen,' Niclas said once he was dressed and laid back on the bed, 'you are far too light and thin.'

'He's right, but I have a remedy for that,' Alcuin said, and left abruptly.

Galen and Niclas were so surprised that they both gazed forlornly at the door. Then Niclas turned and gave Galen a self-conscious smile. Galen wondered what he should do next. It seemed like Niclas was waiting to be dismissed. People rarely deferred to him, though, so he wasn't sure.

'Do... do you know what happened to the gleeman?' Galen asked.

It was something that he'd worried about, after all.

Niclas gave an unexpected derisory tut and said, 'He's turned up at the burh. Banged on the gate yesterday, bold as brass, and demanded entry.'

'So he is still alive,' Galen said. 'I am relieved to hear it.'

'He's a waste of space, if you ask me,' Niclas muttered. 'But I was also glad he made it. He said he hid in the swamp and waited till he was sure the vikings had left, then he came crawling out. Since he was covered in mud from head to foot, I suppose it's true. Hasculf said it's more likely he fell into the marsh and that he's lucky to be alive.'

'Hasculf?'

'The reeve of this burh, Wodenshurst. It's not a bad place, actually. Well run.'

Galen smiled at that. Niclas was typical in that he always thought his home was the best and no other came close. So he'd delivered high, if somewhat grudging, praise.

'Hasculf did say the viking attack was strange, though,' Niclas added. 'They found the hamlet's lookout with his throat cut, which suggests some sort of treachery.'

'Niclas!' Alcuin snapped from the doorway. 'What did I tell you about gossip?'

'Oh, sorry,' Niclas said, and his face took on a stricken expression. 'I'd best go.'

With that, he gave a hurried bow to Galen and rushed off.

'Gossip?' Galen murmured.

'Niclas's tongue tends to run on. I'm trying to get him to keep his mouth shut so that people around here don't learn everything about–'

'I understand.' As usual, Alcuin was doing his best to protect him, and Galen knew full well why. 'But what was this about the lookout?'

'It isn't important.'

'Are you trying to prevent me from worrying?'

'There is nothing we can do about it if there is treachery afoot. I said to Hasculf that the vikings themselves may have come upon the watchman, but he thought it unlikely. They are careful to hide their watch places.

'Whatever the reason, it isn't our business. We just need to get you well enough so we can continue our journey. Which is why I've brought you this.' Alcuin put down a large mug of beer. 'You need to put on weight, and my father says that if there's one thing guaranteed to make a man fat, it's beer.'

'He likes it, does he?' Galen said, eyeing the large mug dubiously.

'All too well,' Alcuin said with a laugh.

'Do you like him? Your father.'

'I like him well enough, but as the youngest son I didn't interest him much.'

'Like my father and me,' Galen said, and took a first tentative sip.

The beer tasted different from the one his mother brewed at home, but it wasn't unpleasant.

'Not entirely. I left home at the age of nine to go to the Monastery of Thurby, so I didn't see my family very much from then. I suppose that's why I'm not that worried about how they feel about me. My mother, till she died, barely saw me or any of us children. She left us with a nurse to bring us up. But I make friends easily, so I didn't repine.'

Galen gave a quick understanding nod, but he felt sad that Alcuin's upbringing hadn't involved a warm family.

Alcuin misunderstood his nod, though, and said, 'Don't think less of yourself for being shy, Galen. People take to you for who you are. They just take a little longer to notice, that's all.'

'I wish I had more courage.'

'Don't,' Alcuin said with a laugh. 'How could I live up to you then?'

'What are you talking about?' Galen asked, for this turn in the conversation made no sense to him.

'How much courage did it take to tell me to go on without you when the vikings were on their way? If that's you being timid, I'd hate to see you being brave.'

'That was different,' Galen said, filled with embarrassment at something he felt foolish about.

'Not really. You see, when it comes down to it, you're as
brave as any other man. Now, I'm glad you've taken a few
sips, but I'm not leaving till you drink all this beer.'

'But I'm full.'

'Make the effort,' Alcuin said and placed the mug back
into Galen's hands. 'I mean it.'

'Then you could be here a long time,' Galen said with a
slight smile. 'Is Niclas not sleeping in this hut with us?'

The wide grin that question got from Alcuin surprised
Galen.

'He daren't.'

This reply was so cryptic that Galen cocked his head to
consider it.

'What is he afraid of?'

'The lesser of his fears is living with you, the son of his
lord and master.'

'That's ridiculous. He slept in my father's long hall, with
my father, brothers and all the thanes.'

'Exactly, all those men, not just you and me. I think he
finds it uncomfortable that it is a small group, and that we
are monks.'

'I see,' Galen said and took another deep draft of beer.
'What's the greater fear?'

'Elves.'

Although Alcuin looked like he was making a joke of
it, Galen sensed he was less than comfortable with the
situation. That was confirmed as Alcuin made a hasty sign
of the cross.

'I have been reliably informed that the previous
occupant spent his last days conversing with a swarm of
elves. So, even though this is the finest house in the burh,
it has remained unoccupied since his death.'

'Ah,' Galen murmured.

Now the charms surrounding him made more sense.

'I don't know what to make of the fact that they put us here,' Alcuin said with a laugh. 'Maybe they think our holy calling will protect us.'

'I suppose so,' Galen said as he put down the now-empty mug.

He didn't want to tie Alcuin to him, so he'd drunk the beer quickly. As he hadn't had anything alcoholic in a while, it made him drowsy and the room became fuzzy. He was vaguely aware of Alcuin pulling him back down and covering him, and then he drifted off to sleep.

CHAPTER 9

When Galen woke, the room was empty, and the only light was that coming from the open doorway. He felt comfortable and at peace, which was unexpected. After all he'd been through, the vikings and his illness, he should have been feeling low, so he couldn't understand it.

The doorway darkened for a moment and a thickset man said, 'May I come in?'

'Yes,' Galen murmured.

He wondered who the man was, still in that relaxed frame of mind that was so unfamiliar to him, especially when meeting strangers. But this man, muscular as he was, seemed safe.

'I'm Hasculf, the shire reeve of this burh.'

'Then I owe you thanks for taking me in.' Surprise flickered across the man's face, and Galen wondered why. 'Are you in the habit of taking in all the wounded that arrive at your gates?'

'I wouldn't turn them away without good reason,' Hasculf said, 'but I would be the least likely to turn you away.'

'Because I'm a monk?'

Galen could think of no other reason.

'Because you rescued my daughter.'

'I did?' Galen said vaguely. 'How... how did I do that?'

'You don't remember?'

Galen forced his mind back, trying to conjure up the events. 'There was a little girl... did she have chestnut hair?'

'That's the one,' Hasculf said. 'After the vikings finished with you, you must have somehow escaped from them and hidden. When Albreda ran past, you pulled her into your hiding place.'

'After the vikings...?' Galen trailed away.

He had no idea what Hasculf was talking about. But he thought it best to ask Alcuin rather than get this stranger to explain.

'Anyway,' Hasculf said, 'I wanted to thank you for rescuing her and for healing her knee.'

'Oh yes?' Galen said, more confused than ever and waiting for Hasculf to explain further, but he didn't.

He murmured another thanks in the manner of a man who wasn't used to being beholden to anyone and respectfully took his leave.

So, when Alcuin arrived with Galen's supper, his face held a deep and puzzled frown.

'Now what's happened?' Alcuin asked.

'I think,' Galen said, watching his friend's face closely, 'I think the people here believe the vikings raped me.'

'Ah! Well, yes, they do.'

'Why? Because I was bleeding?'

'They jumped to the wrong conclusion, and I left them to it. It was easier than trying to explain the truth.'

'They don't seem to mind,' Galen said, which was the greater surprise for him.

'They believe the vikings are capable of any depravity, including raping monks. They were disgusted, but not at you,' Alcuin said and set his tray of food down on the table by Galen's bed.

'Oh.'

'You don't know how that makes you feel.'

'I would have preferred they knew nothing about it. But always being ill the way I am, I suppose some explanation would have been necessary.'

'Ivetta guessed part of the truth, so I confirmed her suspicions, but she hasn't breathed a word to anyone else.'

'Ivetta?'

'She's Hasculf's wife and the burh's healer, a good one at that. She'll come and say hello one day soon, but I told her I'd look after you till you were ready to see other people.'

That explained to Galen why he'd not met any of the townsfolk aside from the reeve. It was typical Alcuin at his most protective and Galen was grateful to him for it.

'And then there's the little girl. Hasculf was talking about me healing her and… whilst I don't remember much of what happened, I'm pretty sure I was in no fit state to heal anyone.'

Alcuin settled on the chair beside Galen and said in an expressionless voice, 'They think you performed a miracle.'

Galen blinked in incomprehension and said, 'A miracle?'

'She had a deformed knee, and after they found her with you, her knee was healed. Albreda thinks you did that.'

'I didn't.'

'I know.'

'The church doesn't like people proclaiming themselves miracle workers,' Galen said nervously.

'I know that too, which is why I've been trying to put paid to this rumour. But there is one thing which appears to be a fact. Somehow, this little girl has gone from having a deformed knee to a normal knee. Even her mother, who is an excellent healer, can't explain that.'

'Oh,' Galen said and took a moment to digest this news. 'Well, it wasn't me.' Alcuin gave less than his usual firm agreement, which made Galen pause. 'What is it?'

'I suppose I've had more time to think about things than you have,' Alcuin said. 'And I have a few questions, that's all.'

'You don't really think I performed a miracle, do you?' Galen was astonished to see his friend's ambivalence.

'When we were at your home, there were two things that made me wonder,' Alcuin said with a slightly embarrassed smile. 'The first was that everyone thought it was a miracle you survived Septimus's attack, especially when nobody else did.'

Galen shook his head, trying to dispel the vision of Septimus squeezing the life out of him, his huge hands wrapped around his throat.

'I was his first, and I look like my father. Maybe he...'

Alcuin waved away the rest of the sentence and said, 'That's what I decided as well, along with everyone else. But then there was the incident with Father Pifus.'

'I really didn't do anything to him,' Galen said.

'But he was trying to push you off the church tower, and he suddenly screamed and dropped you. That made no sense, nor did his subsequent mute state.'

'He took a vow of silence.'

Galen was uncomfortable with the direction this conversation was going.

'For an opinionated man like him?' Alcuin said and shook his head. 'I don't know. That's the thing though, it's the uncertainty. I mean, when we were working on the Life of Saint Cuthbert, all the miracles were so clear. Cuthbert prayed, and then there was an outcome. Here we have three mysterious, unexplained things that you don't want to claim.'

Galen continued to puzzle over this latest development after Alcuin went off for his daily walk. To Galen, it was clear that he'd had nothing to do with anything Alcuin had mentioned. But it worried him that even his friend had his doubts.

Since the autumn was a hot one, he threw back the covers that were now sweltering when added to his robes. Then, working slowly, he pushed himself upright and eased his feet to the floor. The world swam before his eyes for a moment and he sat blinking, trying to clear his vision.

'I don't think you should be doing that,' a young girl said in an imperious tone of voice.

'I have to get up sometime.'

Galen stopped to examine the girl in her pretty deep-blue dress embroidered with a wavy edging of bright yellow thread.

'But Mother hasn't given her permission for you to get up yet,' Albreda said.

'Must she give her permission? I wasn't aware of that,' Galen said with a slight smile.

'Oh, you do smile sometimes,' Albreda said as she ran over to Galen's bed and dropped to her knees beside him.

'Are you Hasculf's daughter?'

'Uh-huh,' Albreda said with a nod. 'You fixed my knee.'

'Did I?' Galen asked, confronted yet again with this mystery.

'Of course you did. And I'm very glad because it isn't sore anymore.'

'Well... that's good, at any rate.'

Galen was trying to feel his way through this conversation and work out what he should tell the girl.

'Brother Alcuin told me that when you woke I mustn't bother you, but you don't mind, do you?'

'No, I don't mind.'

That was true. Galen always felt more comfortable amongst women than with men.

'And you must have sisters, so you know how to talk to girls, don't you?'

'I have four sisters, but they are all older than me.'

'Do you talk to them a lot?'

'As often as I can.'

'I used to talk to my aunt a lot,' Albreda said, and her mood changed to one of deep sadness. 'She was Mother's youngest sister and so much fun, but it looks like the vikings took her.'

'I'm sorry to hear that.'

Despite the strictures of his order, Galen placed his hand on Albreda's shoulder and gave it a squeeze.

'They're going to sell her as a slave, aren't they?' Albreda said. 'And I'll never see her again.'

'We must pray to God to keep her safe,' Galen said. 'And never give up hope that one day you will see her again.'

'Like Mama, she is also being brave,' Albreda said and sniffed her tears away. 'Do you like riddles?'

'Why do you ask me that?'

The change in direction threw Galen, but he thought it might be a good way to cheer Albreda up again.

'Because I like riddles,' Albreda said. 'See if you can guess this one: what walks on four legs in the morning, two legs in the afternoon and three legs in the evening?'

'Ah, that one's easy,' Galen said. 'That is a very ancient riddle, and the answer is a man.'

'Because he crawls on four legs as a baby, walks on two legs as a grownup and when he's old, he has a walking stick,' Albreda said. 'Do you know any other riddles?'

'As it happens, I'm rather fond of riddles, so I know a few.'

Galen looked to the door as he spoke and wondered whether he could make the few paces that would get him there.

'Tell me one!'

'Alright. It's a bit longer than yours and it's describing two things.'

Galen gathered his forces and tried to stand up. He only made it halfway when his strength failed and he dropped back to the bed, panting heavily.

'No!' Albreda said. 'You must not try to stand up, not till Mother says you can. But you can tell me a riddle. I'm very good at guessing riddles.'

Galen was now defeated and more worried than he was going to show this girl about the loss of what little strength he had.

To distract himself as much as amuse Albreda, he said, 'Alright, see what this is:

I saw six creatures scratching at the soil,
their four frolicking sisters pecking round and round.
Pale translucent shell was each of their homes,
and when stripped of their fine gossamer cowls,
none were nude nor raw with pain.
But by God's grace, they quickened and covered and
were brought to grass and grain,
where they picked, strutted and stripped sod.'

'That really is tricky,' Albreda said, crinkling up her face in concentration. 'Tell me again.'

So Galen complied and watched her face whilst she puzzled over the words. Having Albreda around was helpful because she distracted him from an even harder puzzle that he wasn't ready to face yet.

'And you say it's about two things?' Albreda said.

'Two totally different things.'

'Can you give me a clue?'

'Mmm,' Galen said, pretending to give the question some thought by rubbing his hand over his mouth. 'Think about the number of creatures I've mentioned.'

'Ten!'

'So what comes in tens?'

'Fingers! They also have nails like gossamer cowls.'

'There you go. That's the first part of the riddle solved.'

'Now I just need to work out what creatures have shell homes and pick at the ground and... I know!' Albreda said with a laugh. 'It's chickens!'

'Well guessed.'

'That was tricky, though. You're very good at this.'

'It isn't a creation of my own. I heard it from a wandering gleeman when I was a boy.'

'A gleeman arrived here too. I recognised him immediately because of his funny clothes and his ugly face,' Albreda said. 'He came to Tiwham before the vikings did.'

'Tiwham?' Galen realised that the sudden loss of Albreda's sparkle meant she'd gone back to thinking about her aunt. 'Was that the hamlet by the river?'

'Mmm,' Albreda said with a nod. She took a deep breath, and then said in a much more adult way, 'I went with Auntie to visit Ricbert. They were going to get married.'

'I'm sorry.'

Albreda shrugged and said in a distant, trying-to-be-adult, voice, 'Father said the gleeman might help cheer everybody up. But I don't like him.'

It disturbed Galen to hear about Swidhelm from Albreda. His impression of the gleeman had also been negative, although he had no reason for his feeling.

'Is he any good?' he asked, deciding a neutral question would be best.

'He plays the harp very well and tells a good story, but he doesn't do riddles,' Albreda said.

So maybe that was the reason Albreda didn't like him, Galen thought. Children's priorities differed from adults', after all.

CHAPTER 10

G alen sat up in the bed and looked around. He was feeling much stronger today; strong enough that he was going to try to take a walk. It was imperative that he did. There were viking raiders about and a king waiting for them. Both were excellent reasons to be up and back on the road as soon as possible.

Galen decided he'd wait for Alcuin before he attempted that, though, just in case he fell. In the meantime, he felt under his cushions for the small slip of vellum he'd found there a few days before. It was a deep brown colour and had the smooth and greasy texture of something that had been handled for years. For all that, the text was still clear enough to read.

Galen got the impression that the writer had copied the words, shape by shape, with no understanding, from an earlier text. The writing was uneven, and so many errors had crept in over time that it was impossible to work out what some words were even supposed to be.

Galen wasn't surprised. He'd come across charms before. Everybody used them. Farmers hung them in their barns to protect their livestock, midwives kept them for women in labour, and fishermen tied them into their nets to save their nest from ripping

Maybe it was because his mother, a deeply devout woman, had never used charms herself, that Galen felt they weren't necessary. When he was growing up, the children around him had feared elves. Their parents had used that dread to keep them in line. But, fearful as he was as a child, Galen was unconcerned when the thralls looking after them used elves as a threat.

Galen slipped the charm back under the cushion and returned to examining the hut. His mind was in an unsettled state, flitting about from thought to thought. He was living amongst strangers. He'd had a too-close call with vikings. He'd been so near death he'd accepted his fate. There was all the business about a miracle, and he was anxious that their stay in the burh was too long.

With that to spur him on, he pushed himself to eat all he was given. He drank all the beer Alcuin forced on him, and he sat up as much as he could throughout the day. Till finally, he was ready to attempt a short walk.

Alcuin must have thought the same because he arrived with a woman that Galen realised had to be Ivetta. She had a striking resemblance to Albreda.

'I told Ivetta you were much improved and eager to start walking,' Alcuin said with a grin.

Galen felt himself blush. At the same time, he was reassured by Ivetta, who was giving him an understanding smile.

Galen pushed himself onto his feet as he said, 'I am very glad to meet you. Alcuin said he couldn't have healed me without your help.'

'And you already know from Albreda how grateful we are to you,' Ivetta said.

Galen waved the comment away. Then he took a deep breath, gathered his resolve and took his first tentative step. He was embarrassed by how closely both Alcuin and Ivetta were watching him as he made his slow and shaky way to the door. He reached out and put his right hand against the rough wooden frame and took a couple of deep breaths as Alcuin came to stand beside him.

'How does that feel?' Ivetta asked.

Galen half turned his head to give her a smile.

'It's alright. I'm so weak that I'm shaking all over, but that's just from lying down for so long.'

'And from losing all that blood,' Alcuin murmured as he took Galen's elbow to provide him with extra support.

'You're clasping your left arm to your body, so I assume you're still in pain,' Ivetta said.

'Yes.' Galen's gaze slipped to the floor. 'I fear that will always be with me.'

'What a pity. I'm afraid I can think of nothing that will improve the situation.'

'Perhaps the king's leech can do something for me.'

'He must be a very wise man, so no doubt he can achieve more than I or your Brother Benesing could do.'

The doubtful way in which Ivetta spoke prompted Galen to say, 'You don't believe it?'

'I know pride is wrong, but I have yet to hear of any leech who can do more than a mere healer such as myself.'

Galen gave her a regretful smile and said, 'You are probably right. I should try not to build my hopes too high.'

'You have walked about enough for now,' Ivetta said. 'You should sit down again.'

'Just a little longer,' Galen said and glanced outside.

From his bed, all he could see was a corner of another hut. At the door, he was looking out into a small, irregular square, ringed about with houses, and full of livestock and people, refugees from the surrounding hamlets. Many of them were clutching bundles of food or hanging on to a rope that secured one or more of their animals.

Beyond them, and far closer than Galen was used to, was the wooden stockade of the burh. There was a ring of armed men up on the battlement, all facing outwards, watching and waiting. The place was much smaller than his father's burh. That left Galen feeling hemmed in and less secure.

'Ivetta's right, you've had enough for now,' Alcuin said as he pulled Galen from the doorway. 'You must rest now or else you might collapse and do yourself an injury. I don't want to risk it.'

'You can walk a little more later, but not now,' Ivetta said. 'You should pace yourself.'

'I can't just lie about, Madam Ivetta,' Galen said, feeling that he should make more of an effort. 'The king is expecting us and we've kept him waiting long enough.'

'I'm sure the king is expecting many people. Unless you and Brother Alcuin are very important, he probably hasn't even noticed that you aren't there yet.'

Galen was about to tell her not to be foolish when he stopped and said in surprise, 'Oh, you're probably right.'

Ivetta laughed.

'And you are a kind young man. I doubt my husband would have tolerated my speaking to him in that fashion. Now please, sit down.'

Since Galen was feeling very shaky indeed, he was happy to do as he was bid. He allowed Alcuin to walk him back to the bed and ease him down.

'Good,' Ivetta said. 'If you feel strong enough in the next few days, then Brother Alcuin can support you to our long hall one evening for dinner. Alcuin tells me you know Swidhelm who has lately arrived in the burh and Albreda tells me you like gleemen.'

'All I said was that I learned a riddle from one of them, but it will be nice to see something other than these four walls.'

'She's been telling the riddle you set her to all her friends. It's a good one. If you have more, you can share them with us one day.'

Galen had never eaten in any other long hall than his father's. But of one thing he was certain: they had paid him precious little attention at home and he expected the same here.

So, although it gave him a twinge of anxiety, he said, 'I will be glad to go. The walk will be good for me.'

'Just as long as you don't overdo it. However, I know I can trust Brother Alcuin to ensure you don't,' Ivetta said with a knowing smile. 'I am impressed by how well he looks after you.'

Galen nodded an embarrassed agreement. That nearly distracted him from a request he'd been sitting on.

'Um... before you go, Madam Ivetta,' Galen said, 'would it be possible to remove these charms?'

Ivetta looked startled and pointed up at the bundle of herbs hanging over the bed.

'All of them? I really don't think that's safe.'

'God will protect me.'

Galen tried to project the certainty he felt, even though he hated to cause offence to anyone.

Ivetta examined him dubiously but said, 'You would know better than me about that. But the incantations do ask God to protect you from the elves. It isn't like it's a heathen practice.'

'I know, and I thank you for your good intentions. I just... I don't feel comfortable about the charms.'

Galen regretted the words as soon as he'd spoken them because he saw a shift in Ivetta. The charms used to reassure her, and he'd somehow knocked her confidence and faith in them.

'I'm not saying you should stop using them,' he said hastily. 'I don't need them, that's all.'

'Of course,' Ivetta said, but Galen could tell her trust in them was undermined.

She took them all down, though, then gave him and Alcuin a hesitant smile and slight nod, and hurried away.

'Oh dear,' Galen said.

'Do they make you feel that uncomfortable?' Alcuin said as he unfolded the stool and set it up opposite Galen. 'I have to admit they are as familiar to me as a farm implement, so I've never given charms a second thought.'

'They are a comfort to people. I shouldn't have brought that into question. But I don't believe they do any good.'

'Do you think they do harm?' Alcuin said in surprise. 'Are they a tool of the Devil?'

'No,' Galen said, waving away the question. 'If I thought they were harmful, I would have asked for the charms to be removed sooner. I would also have encouraged Ivetta to stop using them. I know how soothing rituals are, though, and the incantations help

Ivetta in her work. I don't want to take that away from her.'

'Mmm,' Alcuin said, and stretched out his legs to get comfortable. 'As usual, you have your own unique view of things. I have a feeling our abbot, or even your Father Pifus, would have been more absolute. They would point out what is right is right and banned people from doing anything else.'

'And yet, Father Pifus never banned the use of charms.'

'Probably because he thought they do protect us against the evil that elves cause.'

Galen nodded agreement.

'What I seldom tell anyone, though,' he murmured, 'is that I don't believe elves exist either.'

Alcuin was so astonished to hear this admission that his eyes bulged, and he sat upright.

'You don't?'

'I don't think I've ever told anyone that before because I expect exactly the reaction I got from you.'

'But Galen, if there are no elves, what brings down misfortune, sickness and even death?'

'I don't know. But ask yourself why the Holy Books never mention elves. And why we never discuss them during our chapter house meetings.'

Alcuin blinked at him as if he were gazing at a stranger.

Then he laughed and said, 'I've never even thought about that. This is why I say you are a wiser man than I am. Very well, I will follow your lead and try to let go of my superstitious belief in elves.'

It astonished Galen every time Alcuin deferred to him. It had a ridiculous air to it. But at least Alcuin had listened

and given his opinion in return and even allowed himself
to be swayed.

CHAPTER 11

G alen eased himself onto the narrow bench outside the house he and Alcuin had lately occupied. It was close enough that he could slip back into the darkness of the hut if he wanted to, which gave him the reassurance he needed to be out alone. He was rather pleased with his first solo walk. In fact, today, he'd waited till Alcuin had left on his usual foray in search of images before he'd made the attempt.

Now he sat in the deep shade provided by the overhanging thatched roof and looked about. It seemed there were more people today than before. He'd lived through two sieges in his father's burh that, thankfully, had come to nothing. People always played it safe, though. They'd head for the burh the moment there was a sign of trouble. Once, there had been a flare-up of tension between his father and a neighbouring ealdorman. The earlier time, barely remembered because Galen had been so young, was when the king had gone to war.

Whenever the people of the hamlets arrived, they were put up in the longhouse and the houses of the residents of the burh. Any spillover had to make do with a lean-to. Wodenshurst was currently dotted about with these shelters. They were just rough branches laid at an

angle against house walls and covered with a layer
of reeds. Entire families and their livestock huddled
inside, making the best of the situation.

Swidhelm strolled into the square, and Galen
watched him with growing curiosity as he picked his
way through the people. He stopped first to chat to the
cobbler. They were out of earshot, so Galen couldn't
hear what was being said. It must have been amusing,
because the cobbler roared with laughter. Swidhelm
patted him on the back and strolled on to the potter to
have a similar conversation.

He looked for all the world like an amiable man
out for a stroll, but Galen didn't believe it. There
was something sharp and prying about the man's gaze.
Swidhelm examined everything more closely and for
longer than a casual observer might.

Galen hoped the gleeman didn't come his way. He
had no wish to talk to him, and he wondered why.
Usually, he enjoyed the tales of anyone who'd travelled
and had insights into the world.

Whispering to his left drew his attention and Galen
discovered that he, too, was being watched. A group of
children had gathered at the bottom of the lane that led
into the square. Albreda stood at the front of the group,
very much the one in charge.

It looked like they wanted to talk to Galen, but were
afraid to do so. They were therefore using Albreda as a
shield for their approach. It astonished Galen. Nobody
had ever been afraid of him before.

'These are my friends,' Albreda announced as she
walked up to Galen. At least she was perfectly at ease. 'The
tall one is Andhun, the girls are Osthrid and Acha, and

the little boy is Hengist. Hengist is from Middleton. His family is taking shelter here now though.'

Hengist nodded solemnly at the introduction. He was wearing a dark green tunic with such long sleeves they'd slipped over his hands and grazed the ground.

He gazed up at Galen and said with a lisp caused by a missing front tooth, 'Did you really save Albreda's life?'

'He did,' Albreda said, giving the boy a push. 'Why are you asking about something you already know?'

'Because he's too scared to ask him for a miracle,' the red-headed Osthrid said.

'Do you want a miracle?' Galen asked, because he felt he should at least take part in the conversation.

'Can you set something on fire just by looking at it?' Hengist asked, his eyes bright with excitement.

'I can't,' Galen said with a slight, regretful smile. 'And that's not exactly a miracle, is it? Miracles are done for good reasons.'

'It would be good if you set a viking ship on fire,' Hengist said with dogged determination.

Fortunately, Galen was saved from replying when the shy-looking Acha asked, 'How about talking to ravens like Saint Cuthbert, can you do that?'

'I can't do that either.'

'That's not much of a miracle,' Hengist snorted. 'Why would you want to speak to a raven?'

'Well,' Galen said, 'in the case of Saint Cuthbert, it was because the ravens were stealing the thatch from his roof and the roofs of all the villagers. So he told them they were harming the people, and they flew off.'

'That still doesn't sound very miraculous. My dad is always shouting at the ravens and the crows who steal our thatch. It doesn't stop them.'

'Saint Cuthbert was more successful. Not only did the ravens stop stealing the thatch, but they returned and spread themselves on the ground in apology. Then they gave Cuthbert a lump of lard that he could use to grease his shoes and the shoes of his guests.'

Hengist looked thoroughly unimpressed by what he clearly thought was a trivial miracle. It made a part of Galen wish he could do something spectacular for these children so they wouldn't leave disappointed. But he had nothing he could do.

'I'm afraid I have no powers at all.'

'So how come you could hide from the vikings?' Andhun asked, finally breaking his silence. 'And how come you fixed Albreda's knee? She used to limp and now she doesn't.'

The cluster of children gathered around him nodded unanimously at that question.

'Whatever happened to Albreda was done by God's will. I didn't do it,' Galen said.

'Oh,' Osthrid said, swaying back and forth in front of Galen. 'So you can't do anything interesting?'

'I'm afraid not.'

'Oh, well...' Hengist wiped his snotty nose with one outrageously long sleeve and wandered away, trailed by all the others except Albreda.

She smiled up at Galen and said, 'I know you performed a miracle.'

Galen decided there was no point in trying to correct her iron-clad conviction.

'Then you should thank God for what happened.'

'I do. But I also thank you, because you saved me from the vikings.'

Galen nodded acceptance. He supposed he had done that. Then his attention was caught by Swidhelm again. He seemed to be creeping down the street as if he didn't want to be spotted.

'He goes about everywhere like that,' Albreda said as she followed Galen's gaze.

'Does he?'

'He's always snooping and peeping and looking at everything. Father said he's tired of him and that I have to stay away from him.'

So Hasculf had noticed Swidhelm's behaviour, too. It relieved Galen to hear it.

'I suppose you could say the same for Brother Alcuin. He's also always looking around,' Galen said, by way of a test.

'It isn't the same at all,' Albreda said. 'Brother Alcuin always asks permission before he draws anything.'

'I see.'

This confirmed to Galen's own satisfaction that Swidhelm was going beyond what a casual observer might do. He was about to ask Albreda what else the gleeman had been up to, when the women of the burh emerged and started calling their children home.

'Dinner!' Albreda said, grinning broadly at Galen before she dashed off.

Her words reminded Galen that he'd agreed, this very morning, to go to the long hall for dinner. His hands shook with sudden fright. He felt the nausea building in his gut at the thought of having to sit in a room full of strangers.

Why had it seemed like a good idea when he'd been invited by Ivetta only a few hours ago?

CHAPTER 12

Galen dearly wanted to pull out of going to the hall but, at the same time, he didn't want to look like a coward. He'd found it incomprehensible that Alcuin thought him brave. Just as he'd dismissed his father's words to the same effect. But he didn't want to lose the esteem he'd somehow gained.

So, as Alcuin came strolling back to their hut and said, 'Are you ready?' Galen forced a smile and stood up.

'I'm as ready as I'll ever be.'

Alcuin knew him so well he gave him an understanding smile, took Galen by the elbow and said, 'Lean on me as much as you need. And, whatever you do, don't strain yourself. We don't want a relapse on our hands.'

'No, of course not,' Galen said mechanically as he stepped out into the square and noted that it was devoid of people. Only the livestock remained. He guessed that everyone else must have gone to the hall. That realisation brought on a tremor of fright.

'Are you sure you're up to this?' Alcuin said, and his grip on Galen's arm tightened.

'I'm just a little nervous,' Galen said, and felt his face prickle with embarrassment. 'I don't know these people.'

'Well, they're all very well disposed towards you, so don't worry,' Alcuin said. 'You have grown in status in this burh for two reasons: first as a worker of miracles. I might not approve of the first reason, but I am fine with the second.'

'What is that?' Galen asked, more for a distraction than because he wanted to know.

He worried about the rumour of the miracle and the fact that it would spread beyond the burh once all the refugees went home.

'They think you are a man of learning. I guess it's because of the riddle Albreda spread to everyone. Either way, they are not mistaken in that.'

Galen laughed and shook his head.

'You should brace yourself for a warm welcome,' Alcuin said, accepting Galen's dismissal of his words. 'I doubt your arrival anywhere else has ever been greeted with as much anticipation.'

Galen found that hard to believe. He knew how insignificant he was. And yet, as he and Alcuin stepped into the long hall crammed with people, a cheer went up and everyone rose to their feet.

'Welcome, Brother Galen,' Hasculf said as he held up his mug in salute. 'Welcome to Wodenshurst and our hearth.'

Galen was astonished as he looked around the hall. There were hundreds of smiling faces illuminated by dozens of torches.

'Thank... thank you,' he murmured, almost too overwhelmed to speak.

'Let's get you to a seat,' Alcuin said. 'You'll be on Hasculf's right in the place of honour.'

'Oh no, I couldn't–' Galen said and then realised that the hall had fallen silent and everyone was listening to him and Alcuin.

'He'll be offended if you don't,' Alcuin murmured in his ear.

He steered Galen to the table that took pride of place in the centre of the hall before the hearth fire and helped him sit.

'Welcome,' Hasculf said, as Galen sat down and gave him an apprehensive look. 'I am very pleased that you could join us.'

Galen nodded and cast another quick glance around the space. He had never seen a fuller hall. Men were packed so tightly on the benches they jostled elbows. But the ones that had found a seat were the lucky ones. Dozens more stood in the empty gaps between the tables, all watching Galen.

Hasculf laughed at his bewilderment and shouted, 'Bring out the food. And the best mead for Brother Galen!'

The women arrived at a run, weaving between the men, their trays full of roast meat, sausages and pies. Others came laden with bread and a third group poured the drinks.

After the initial shock, Galen realised he was being watched by everyone in a benevolent way. Alcuin had been right. They were glad to see him. He was more used to passing unnoticed, or, at worst, having people whisper and look disapproving. Here, he truly felt like a guest of honour.

Alcuin sat to Galen's right and beamed at him, as if to say, 'See!'

'You don't have a priest?' Galen said to Hasculf while the women filled everybody's plates.

'We are too small a burh to support one. But there is a wandering priest who does the rounds between us and several local hams.'

'I see,' Galen said, uncertain of what to say next.

'I usually say grace,' Hasculf said, understanding Galen. 'And since his arrival, Brother Alcuin has done so for us. But tonight I would be glad if you gave us a blessing.'

Galen had a sinking feeling they made the request because of his reputation as a miracle worker, but he was too intimidated by the waiting crowd and the reeve to turn it down. So he forced a smile and nodded acceptance. He supposed it would be easier to give a blessing in this friendly place than it had been in his father's more watchful hall.

'Silence!' Hasculf shouted. 'All rise for the blessing.'

He turned to Galen, who had no choice but to push himself to his feet and hold his hand out over the crowd.

'Dear God, our Father, as the harvest comes to an end, I thank You for the bountiful crops. I pray You keep this burh and all its people safe from marauders during these dangerous times. And I pray that You shine Your blessing down on Hasculf and his people, who are so welcoming to strangers. Amen.'

'Amen,' the hall chimed, and then a cheer went up.

'Thank you,' Hasculf said as he sat back down. 'I am reassured about the future now.'

'Even so,' Galen murmured, 'with the threat of vikings so near, should you be holding such a lavish feast?'

'It's good for morale. And worth it for all you have done for us.'

Galen wanted to urge him not to be complacent and to reiterate that he was no saint and incapable of protecting the burh. But he bit back the words. At least Hasculf was happy for now. To provide even momentary relief from their fears was the least Galen could do. Especially when he and Alcuin were being looked after so well.

So he nodded and turned his attention to the immense plate of food they had given him. He doubted even his father, whose appetite was prodigious, could have worked his way through such a helping. He picked up a meat-covered bone and bit into it. As he chewed, he felt safe to look around. It didn't surprise him that he was still the centre of attention. Fragments of what was being said drifted up to him.

'He's very modest.'

'Just as a saint should be.'

'I thought he'd be bigger.'

'No need if God is protecting him.'

Galen's heart sank to hear those snatches of conversation. The townspeople thought his behaviour was appropriate to what they'd expect from a saint.

Ivetta must have seen the dismay on his face and, he realised, on Alcuin's.

She said to Alcuin as she topped up his drink, 'They can't help it. Especially as two miracles are being whispered about.'

'Don't tell me the baby's club foot has been healed.'

Galen wondered what baby they were talking about. He was certain he'd not been anywhere near a baby.

'No,' Ivetta said, 'but I had very little hope that the boy would live, never mind his deformity. Now he's well on the road to recovery. I believe he will grow up, after all.'

'That surely isn't down to Galen,' Alcuin said, and Galen agreed with him.

'Why not? Why are you, a man of the church, a man who should believe in miracles, so reluctant to believe this of Brother Galen?'

'I am no more reluctant than Galen is himself,' Alcuin said and turned to his friend. Galen nodded agreement. 'And in these times it is best not to stir up talk of miracles.'

'Because the end is near?' Ivetta asked.

'Some fear that is so.'

Galen decided against chiming in. He'd had a similar conversation with his mother and heard it often enough at the abbey, too. He didn't think the end was near. But he also knew that people were so afraid that they wouldn't, or couldn't, listen to him when he gave his opinion.

'When the Last Judgement comes, we have been told many strange things will happen,' Ivetta said. 'That bright star streaking across the heavens in years past was the first sign. But there will be others, and perhaps Brother Galen is another of those signs.'

Galen shook his head, but Ivetta and Alcuin were so absorbed in their conversation they didn't notice.

'Along with all the viking attacks?' Alcuin said.

'They are heathens and they test us at this important time. Hasculf said he is expecting another raiding party. The vikings sometimes send out a smaller party to test the people before they come back with a bigger group.'

'Maybe you're right,' Alcuin said, and then stopped because Galen had rammed him in his side with his elbow.

'They're just people,' Galen muttered. 'Don't build too much into it.'

He didn't want to argue with Alcuin and was relieved when Hasculf shouted, 'Where's Swidhelm? It's time to earn your keep, gleeman. Get out your harp and sing us a few songs.'

'I am here,' Swidhelm said as he rose from a corner bench, stepped out to the centre of the hall, before the fire, and took a bow. 'And I am always ready to entertain my fellow man. Perhaps I can start with an epic poem.'

And so he began reciting a poem and accompanying the events with his harp. Sometimes he played a sweet melody for a scene of kindness. Other times, he strummed it vigorously to simulate a clash of arms from a mighty battle.

Galen was absorbed, not just by the tale itself, but by the way it was being told. He hoped it would be a truly epic poem but, in the end, it wasn't as long as he'd expected. Swidhelm played a final chord, bowed low, and rode the cheers. Then he held up his hand for quiet.

'Gentlefolk, it isn't often that I am upstaged, but I am as intrigued by Brothers Alcuin and Galen as the rest of you are. They have been involved in a stirring adventure which I am sure will be worked into a saga one day.'

Galen's eyes flew to Alcuin's as they looked at each other in dismay.

'But such serious matters can wait,' Swidhelm said with a big grin, 'for I hear that Brother Galen is a master of riddles, too.'

Everyone turned expectantly to Galen, while he flushed a deep red and stared at his plate.

'What do you say, Brother Galen?' the gleeman asked. 'Will you test us with a riddle?'

'I... I don't know,' Galen muttered.

'We'd be very pleased if you did,' Hasculf said. 'The one you taught Albreda has already been shared around the burh.'

'Well,' Galen said, and searched his memories for a riddle.

'Here's one:

I am a wonder to women, a help for times to come.
I harm none but my slayer.
I stand rooted on a high bed, shaggy hair at my base.
Sometimes the maiden grasps me eagerly, sometimes the rich old woman grabs hard hold of my body.
They push back my red skin, claim my proud head.
The curly-haired wanton who catches me fast will feel our meeting.
Her eye will be wet.'

Stunned silence filled the hall for a moment as Galen finished. He flushed a deeper red and hung his head as he wondered whether it was a good choice after all. It was one of his most popular riddles, for good reason. But now that he'd spoken it out loud before this crowd of strangers, he was regretting it.

Hasculf roared with sudden laughter.

'Who would have thought such a saintly-looking young man would come out with such a riddle? But it is far too easy, my friend. You must try another.'

'No,' Galen said, 'don't let its simplicity trick you or you will make the wrong guess.'

'But it's a dick!' Odo shouted from the far end of the room. 'Anyone can see that.'

'You are mistaken.'

'It isn't a dick?' Hasculf said as a pleased smile spread across his face. 'Well then, let's see, what can it be…? Recite it again.'

Galen obliged several times, rejecting all the guesses that grew wilder and a good bit lewder as the night progressed.

Finally, Hasculf said, 'I give up. What is it?'

'I will answer you with another riddle,' Galen said. 'It describes exactly the same thing as the last.'

'Ah, a clue, go ahead,' Hasculf said, his eyes gleaming with amusement.

'Alright,' Galen said.

'I say nothing, I am a stalk of the living.
I say nothing, I stand waiting to join the dead.
I rose before, I will rise again.
Though plunderers carve and split my skin,
though plunderers bite through my bare body,
shear my head and hold me hard in a slicing bed.
I bite no man unless he bites me,
but the numbers who bite are many.'

'Mmm, it seems to me it's some sort of food.'

'Yes,' Galen said with a smile.

Swidhelm snapped his fingers as a look of great cunning came into his eyes.

'Could it be that we are talking of an onion?'

'Yes, that's it,' Galen said.

'Ha! That was very well done, Brother Galen,' Hasculf said. 'I don't remember when last we were so tested by a riddle.'

CHAPTER 13

G alen was so surprised by the events of the evening that he barely noticed the people as he sat on the bench outside the hut the following morning. Never in his life had he been so feted. The burh had treated him like the most honoured person in the hall.

It was a seductive experience. Galen now understood how it could be so appealing that it encouraged people to put themselves forward to get even more of the attention. He didn't think he'd be able to do that. Much as he'd enjoyed being at the centre of the party, it was exhausting at the same time.

There was also the new and unaccustomed dread in the pit of his stomach that the adulation could slip away with one careless word or foolish gesture. No, it was safer to remain in the background. It was better not to attract attention at all.

He would leave popularity to people like Alcuin, who didn't care so much about what people thought of him. Alcuin had an effortless charm. He could laugh off a snub, or win back friends with his easy smile if he said anything that offended people. Not that he ever did.

It had been Alcuin, with his grace and his self-assurance, who had got Galen out of the hall without offending his hosts, when he'd seen his friend flagging. Galen would have liked to have left even sooner, but he'd had no idea how to do it. Not when he was the centre of attention. His usual method of slipping away unobserved simply wouldn't have worked.

Galen was so absorbed in his own thoughts that he didn't realise somebody had approached him till he noticed their feet right before him.

'Good morning, sir,' the cobbler said and gave a deep bow.

'Good morning,' Galen said and resisted the temptation to tell the man not to bow. It would only lead to a tangle of explanations and further miscommunication. 'Master Bertwald, isn't it?'

'You know my name?' the man said, colouring as if he'd had a great honour bestowed upon him.

'We have been neighbours for a while, haven't we?' Galen said, to prevent the man from treating his knowledge like some saintly mystery. 'I've heard people calling your name.'

'Ah,' the man said, nodding as he chewed on his shaggy moustache. 'I see. I have been wanting to thank you. The child... the child with the club foot is my grandson.'

'I don't remember meeting him.'

Galen wracked his brain for something to dissuade this man from taking further leaps of imagination about something he claimed no responsibility for.

'You were unconscious at the time. But Brother Alcuin put your hand on Bercthun's head and now he is much improved,' Bertwald said, rocking back and forth on his heels, his hands behind his back.

'I am glad to hear he is better, but–'

'I made you these by way of thanks,' Bertwald said and held out a pair of shoes before him, flushing even deeper red as he did so.

'Shoes? Thank you, but there really is no need,' Galen murmured.

'Your shoes look worn, and you have a long journey ahead of you,' Bertwald said. 'I will trade your old shoes for the new ones.'

'I hardly walk at all and my current–'

'Please accept them. I was sure Bercthun was going to die, and that would have killed my daughter too. No good comes from losing your firstborn.'

Galen sighed, but felt he couldn't refuse this request.

'Alright, then I thank you for your gift.'

Bertwald nodded. Then, with a muttered apology, he knelt down, undid Galen's shoes and replaced them with the new ones. 'I softened the leather as much as I could. They should wear in quickly.'

'Thank you,' Galen said, overwhelmed by this man's kindness.

Bertwald nodded and turned to leave.

'Wait,' Galen said. 'When your grandson is old enough, you should send him to a monastery. Boys like him and like me... we can't become warriors, but we can be scholars.'

'Do you think he could be as clever as you?'

'Why not?' Galen said with a shrug. 'All it takes is a bit of learning.'

He watched the cobbler cross the square back to his shop and decided the man looked relieved. Either he was glad he'd completed the trial of handing over the gift, or he saw a way for his grandson to have a decent future.

Galen wondered which it was. He would have considered it more deeply, but Swidhelm arrived in the square. To Galen's dismay, the gleeman, realising he was spotted, made straight for him. It appeared, now that the locals had all met him, they were going to visit. Not that Swidhelm was a local, nor a welcome presence.

'So you are now the famous Brother Galen,' the gleeman said as he sat down, rocking the bench.

'I'm not famous.'

Galen was uncomfortable with his closeness and the smirking way in which Swidhelm had spoken.

'But you will be. Curing a girl with a deformed knee is worth at least a small saga, especially when you rescued that same girl from viking raiders.'

'We were just lucky.'

'Ah, so you are modest too.'

'Please, don't spread this story about.'

Galen had no wish for renown. But he also feared that information about the rest of his life would follow the story.

'But why not tell people?' Swidhelm said. 'In these troubled times, yours is a story of hope.'

'No, it isn't. It was just an accident, please.'

'What are you so afraid of?' Swidhelm said, and his eyes narrowed to calculating slits.

Galen felt helpless before the gleeman. Swidhelm was eager, like a dog trying to dig out a rat. He bristled with suspicion that someone, anyone, might not want to be a character in an ode of his making.

'The people of this burh are simple. They believe a miracle happened when it didn't. There is nothing more to the tale than that.'

'So you say. But it is still a good story. That and your riddles. I haven't heard riddles of such subtlety for a long time.'

'They aren't my riddles. I was repeating what I'd heard from others in my father's hall.'

'So you are the son of a noble.'

'I am,' Galen said, and his discomfort grew.

It was a short step from that to finding out his father's name and then all the rest.

'You are strangely modest,' Swidhelm said.

Galen wished the man would go away. He was frantically trying to find any words that would drive him off when Alcuin arrived.

'My friend needs to rest. You'd best move on now.'

Swidhelm jumped to his feet, swept a bow, gave Alcuin an obsequious smile and said, 'Of course, my lord.'

Galen sighed with relief as he watched the man leave and said, 'Thank you. I couldn't get him to go.'

'That's because you're too kind,' Alcuin said as he sat down. 'You didn't want to hurt his feelings.'

'It wasn't only that. You sounded so implacable and impossible to resist.'

'Well, I was,' Alcuin said with a grin. 'Because if he hadn't left of his own free will, I would have hauled him up by his shirt and breeches and hurled him out.'

Galen laughed.

'That would have been a fine thing to see, even if I don't think we monks should be so violent.'

'Only where it's appropriate. And believe me, that gleeman has been making himself obnoxious with everyone in the burh. I wouldn't be surprised if Hasculf chucked him out soon.'

'He might cause trouble. I fear he'll spread this story of a miracle. I tried to shake him off, but it only made him more curious.'

'I wouldn't worry about it. Nobody of importance will pay any heed to what that gleeman has to say.'

Galen prayed that Alcuin was not just saying something to reassure him.

'I am sure you are right.'

'Do you know, Galen, you are far cleverer than me. You shouldn't be so willing to accept my words as if I am an older and wiser head and deserve to be believed.'

Galen was so surprised by that comment that he said, 'What?'

Alcuin smiled ruefully and said, 'I'm a cheerful fellow and easy-going. I can draw well, but I'm not a deep thinker. That's you.'

'No.'

'I'm afraid so. What you see on my surface - my pretty face and my pretty art - that's all I have. But Abbot Dyrewine told me he'd give scribing to you over any other because you can always find the best way with words. You can mend bad translating, you make up acrostics and remember damned tricky riddles. You are a very brainy fellow.'

'But you have charm. You can get people to do things for you, even me.'

'Like that's so difficult,' Alcuin said with a grin.

'Well, no, it isn't,' Galen said, blushing and looking away.

'I didn't mean it as an insult. All I was trying to say is... well, you have more brains than me. You should be the one telling me what we should do, not the other way around.'

'I don't want to,' Galen said, feeling increasingly unsettled by the conversation.

'Don't worry about it. We handsome, charismatic people seldom allow others to overrule us, even when, in our hearts, we know we should. Now, how do you feel about a little walk if I give you my arm to lean on?'

'That's a good idea,' Galen said, and allowed himself to be hoisted to his feet by Alcuin. 'We've been here too long, haven't we?'

'We've been here as long as was necessary,' Alcuin said as he guided Galen down a path he had yet to explore.

'Too long,' Galen said, picking his way past the lounging refugees that turned the path into an obstacle course.

'Galen—' Alcuin said and stopped his slow walk to turn and face his friend, 'I thought you were going to die. The only people I've seen in as bad a way as you, did die. You are your own little miracle because this is probably the second time you've cheated death. That's not even including the wonder that the vikings didn't see you when you were right beside the road in that log pile.'

Galen blinked in surprise at Alcuin.

'What are you saying?'

'Just that nobody rises from their deathbed and heads off in a rush to Lundenburh. If I have to, I'll explain to the king what took us so long. But I'll be damned if I push you into a tiring journey before you're strong enough to manage it. I've had enough of a fright as it is.'

'Sorry.'

'It's alright, but there you've just had a display of my bullying behaviour. Now, don't you dare try to tell me you're cleverer and we have to leave soon for some good reason or other, because I'll just ignore you.'

'I won't,' Galen said with a slight, embarrassed smile, and checked the faces of the nearby people to see whether they'd been overheard. It didn't seem as if they had.

'Fine. In that case, I'll take you to see our cart. Hasculf's men have been hard at work repairing it. And the women of the burh have sewn the canopy together again and fixed it back on its frame. It looks as good as new. Which was a relief to Niclas.'

'What of his mule?'

'Fortunately, he was found as well. He'd thrown a shoe, so that's also been fixed, and he'll be able to get us all the way to Lundenburh.'

Alcuin and Galen rounded a corner and the view opened up into the semi-circular space in front of the burh's main gates. A pair of men stood on the inside of the closed gates, watching the monks' approach. One of the men was Odo, who waved a casual salute at them. Another dozen men were spread along an upper walkway of the wall, all looking outwards across the flat land.

'There's our cart,' Alcuin said of the vehicle that was pulled up alongside the massive wooden timbers of the burh's defensive wall.

Usually, it looked quite big with its canopy, but the wall dwarfed it.

'This is quite a defensive structure. It's higher than my father's fortifications,' Galen said.

'From everything I've heard, they need it here. The town of Grantabrycge is further upriver and was invaded and settled by Danes about a hundred years ago. Hasculf recommends we avoid it on our way to Lundenburh.'

'Are they that dangerous?' Galen said. 'I thought the settled Danes had accepted God into their hearts and sworn allegiance to the king.'

'They have accepted God. But Hasculf suspects they are less loyal to the king, although he wasn't explicit. They are his neighbours, after all. He trades with them and, on occasion, they have united against the common enemy of the raiding vikings.'

Alcuin guided Galen up to the cart and gave one of the repaired struts a shove to test its strength.

'Hasculf has sent word to Grantabrycge about the latest viking attack. He's also opened a dialogue about mutual support, although he has yet to hear back about that.'

'It is a complex situation.'

Galen was about to ask more when he spotted Swidhelm sneaking through the shadows of a house opposite. He squeezed Alcuin's arm as a warning and turned them away so that Swidhelm couldn't overhear them.

'It's the gleeman again,' Galen murmured.

'Snooping?' Alcuin said and turned his head to look.

Galen wanted to shout at him not to. Instead, he asked, 'Is he still there?'

'He's slipped off down one of the other paths that leads along the wall.'

'You may think I'm overreacting, but I don't want to travel with Swidhelm when we leave. I don't trust him.'

'Neither do I,' Alcuin said as he leaned against the side of their cart and waited for Galen to do the same. 'What is it about him that worries you?'

'It's his accent,' Galen said, relieved that he could rest not only against the cart, but in the shade it provided.

'Mostly, he sounds like us. But last night in the hall, his accent slipped and now and then he sounded like a Dane.'

'Mmm,' Alcuin said, nodding thoughtfully. 'I wondered what that was. I noticed a slight difference too. What else?'

'The saga he was recounting. There were a couple of mentions of a one-eyed king. One of the Danish gods has one eye, so I think he was telling us a Danish tale. I have no problem with that, but it made me wonder more about Swidhelm.'

'They have a one-eyed god?'

'He's their leader.'

'Did you read about that?'

Galen shook his head and said, 'The Danes don't tend to put things into books. They hand their stories down from one generation to the next by word of mouth. That's how I learned some of their lore too, from a visiting gleeman.'

CHAPTER 14

Alcuin wasn't going to show Galen that his observations about Swidhelm made himself nervous, too. First, because of Galen's anxious temperament and his anxiety about keeping the king waiting. Second, because neither of them had been under threat of a viking attack before.

Alcuin realised how fortunate they were when he heard the hair-raising tales of Hasculf and his people. They'd seen off multiple viking raids over the years. They acted as if it were just a way of life, but the strain in their eyes told a different tale.

Alcuin wished he could change the situation, but there really was nothing he could do. He was still haunted by the one battle he'd been involved in. He now feared he'd be called upon to do something like that again.

He also realised that, short of leaving their land and moving west, Hasculf's people would always be at the mercy of the vikings. Their only other hope was that the ransom King Aethelred paid the vikings would keep the worst of the raiders from their shores.

His fears invaded his dreams and, after tossing and turning for hours, his final thought before he dropped off was that he and Galen had to get away as soon as possible.

'Alcuin! Alcuin!' Galen whispered into his ear while his hand gripped Alcuin's arm, shaking him awake.

'Huh, what is it?' Alcuin asked and looked about the dark hut blearily.

It felt like he'd only just fallen asleep.

'Swid... Swidhelm was here,' Galen gasped.

That sent a jolt through Alcuin that not only woke him up but launched him to his feet.

'What?' He only just made that a whisper rather than a shout. He had no wish to wake the neighbourhood nor alarm Galen even more. 'What was he doing?'

'I don't know exactly. But he woke me as he was cutting a piece of my hair off.'

Galen pulled at the hair near his temple. Even in the dark of the hut, Alcuin could see where Swidhelm had sawn away a sizeable chunk.

'The devil! What did he want that for?'

'I don't know,' Galen murmured as he wrapped his arms around himself and shuddered.

'Well, nobody goes after my friend. Wait here. I'm going to find him.'

'No, Alcuin, it might be dangerous,' Galen called after him.

Alcuin was too enraged to heed him and ran out into the night. It was still dark, but the faintest of light in the sky hinted that dawn was on the way. Alcuin looked about the small square, but could only see a multitude of sleeping bodies and slumbering livestock. Then the sound of someone tripping, followed by a muffled curse, drew his attention. It was coming from a path that led to the burh wall.

Alcuin ran full tilt towards the sound and hit the same obstacle. He went flying, rolled over, and gingerly felt his shins. They hurt so much he had to shove his arm into his mouth to prevent a string of curses. It felt like he'd run into the pole from a lean-to that was just a dim shadow, barely visible in the dark alley.

He had no time to feel sorry for himself, though. Alcuin scrambled back onto his feet and half hobbled, half ran down the path. He'd walked every one of the burh's lanes, so he knew this one went to the wall more or less on the opposite side to the main gate.

Alcuin slowed as he reached the end of the lane. There was a clear ring free of houses on the inside of the wall. He moved as slowly and quietly as he could and peeked out. He was in time to see a shadow sneaking up the ladder that led to the upper gangway.

He looked around for a guard and was surprised not to see one. He contemplated making a racket to at least draw some attention. Then he decided he didn't want Swidhelm to know he was being followed yet. He was pretty certain the figure going up the ladder was the gleeman. Alcuin waited till Swidhelm was all the way up before he dashed across the gap to the ladder and climbed to the top.

There was nobody in sight; just a few barrels and some supplies covered by rough sacking. A thin yellow band was visible on the horizon, which made it easier to see. Alcuin crept up to the edge of the wall and looked over the top.

A man was expertly slipping his way down the wall with the help of a rope. He had a harp rather incongruously slung over his shoulder. So it was Swidhelm. Alcuin wondered whether he should cut the rope. That would cause quite a drop for Swidhelm and, most likely, an injury. The other option was to try to haul him back in.

His dislike of the man tempted him to the former. His lack of a knife decided him. He'd haul him in.

Alcuin reached for the rope and was about to give it a heave when a heavy hand gripped his shoulder. It was only by God's grace that Alcuin didn't give a shout of surprise. Glaring at him from underneath some sacking, his finger on his lips, was Hasculf.

'What are you doing?' Alcuin mouthed.

He became aware that much of what he'd thought were supplies were actually the burh's guards. They were peering out at him from under various disguises and watching with a mixture of exasperation and amusement. Then two of the men peeped over the edge and gave an all-clear sign.

'You knew he was going to do that?' Alcuin whispered.

'He isn't the first spy we've had come through our burh,' Hasculf murmured. 'The vikings aren't stupid. They prepare in advance, especially with fortified burhs like ours. So we watch every stranger we let in, just in case.'

'Does that include me and Galen?'

'We have watched you too, although we were far less suspicious of a pair of monks, since the vikings have no love of religious men. And Brother Galen rescued Albreda. I know that wasn't some made-up tale. So I trust you. Although I would have had my doubts if you'd gone over the wall after Swidhelm.'

'I would never have left Galen behind,' Alcuin said. 'But this is surely not so common for you, having a man go over the wall.'

'He was somewhat stuck,' Hasculf said, and his teeth shone white as he flashed a grin that was echoed by the surrounding men. 'We closed the gates, you see. Usually, a spy comes in, looks around pretending to be a trader or some such, and then leaves. We follow them and sometimes discover whom they hand their information over to and where. Then we take the necessary precautions.'

'Only sometimes?'

'We aren't always right about the people we suspect. And occasionally a spy has been so subtle that we've lost them, or missed how or when they informed on us. But we catch them often enough.'

'But this time your gates have been shut in anticipation of an attack.'

'Exactly. And that's why we were even more suspicious of the gleeman when he came banging on our door. He could and should have carried on further inland to greater safety.'

'So it wasn't just because he was annoying that you disliked him.'

'I've had my doubts about him from the start.'

'The same as Galen,' Alcuin said with an introspective laugh.

'The saint suspected Swidhelm?'

It seemed to Alcuin that Galen rose yet again in Hasculf's estimation.

'He did, although he'll not thank you for calling him a saint.' To prevent further exploration of a theme he wasn't keen on anyway, Alcuin asked, 'How did you know Swidhelm would make his escape here?'

'Because we knew he'd need to get out to tell his allies all about us, so we set up a little hole for him to escape through. All the while he's been here, we've made it look like we're careless about this section of our wall. A proper warrior would have been suspicious of this gap. But Swidhelm drinks too much and thinks he's clever, so he didn't realise it's a trap.'

'But he's out, and you didn't send men after him.'

'We've had men waiting outside for him to appear since he got here. Don't worry, he won't get away.'

Alcuin laughed and said, 'I'm glad you're so well prepared. It has set my mind at rest. Now I'd better get back to Galen. He'll be fretting about me.'

'He likes you a lot. You are a fortunate man. But why were you chasing after Swidhelm in the first place?'

'Ah,' Alcuin said, finally with a piece of news of his own. 'Swidhelm snuck into our house and stole a lock of Galen's hair.'

Hasculf swore to hear it, and the surrounding men looked equally perturbed.

'Why? What's the matter?' Alcuin asked.

'With the vikings, I'd say there's devilry afoot,' Hasculf said. 'No doubt they will try to weave a spell using Galen's hair that will advantage them and cause us harm.'

'Perhaps.' That prospect did alarm Alcuin, but he felt he had to do what he could to reassure Hasculf and his men. 'But while they may have a few of Galen's hairs, we've got the rest of him.'

His words worked like magic, and Alcuin saw the tension leave the men. He decided now was the best time to withdraw before he said anything to undermine their new confidence. So he gave them a nod of farewell, scrambled down the ladder and hurried back to the house he and Galen had made their own.

Galen was standing in the doorway, peering out anxiously into the dawn.

'Alcuin, thank God,' he said as he spotted his friend.

'Why are you so worried?' Alcuin said, grinning at him.

'Because you are unarmed and you ran off into the night after a man with a dagger. I shouldn't have let you do that.'

'Idiot,' Alcuin said, and gave Galen's arm a friendly punch. 'Come on back to bed, the sun may be up, but it's still far too early to be awake.'

'Did you find Swidhelm?' Galen asked as he allowed Alcuin to guide him back to the bed.

'Swidhelm went over the wall.'

Because Alcuin knew Galen wouldn't be satisfied with that cryptic response, he relayed the rest of what had happened and everything Hasculf had told him.

'They laid a trap?' Galen said in wide-eyed amazement once Alcuin had finished his tale.

'They did indeed. It seems the reeve has earned every bit of his people's respect with his cunning.'

'He is a good man. Does he really think the vikings will use my hair for a spell?'

'There's no doubt about it. But as I told him, we have you,' Alcuin said and watched the thoughts flicker across Galen's all-too-expressive face. He wasn't thrilled, but he also looked resigned.

'If I can reassure the people, then I suppose it was worth doing,' Galen murmured. 'I just pray I don't let them down, for, as you and I know, I have no saintly powers.'

Chapter 15

The fact that Swidhelm had gone over the burh walls made the viking threat feel that much closer. As Galen sat on his little bench watching and sipping on his huge mug of beer, people clustered in groups, gossiping and looking about fearfully. Even the children were more subdued and stuck close to their parents.

The men pacing back and forth on the burh wall above looked extra alert and filled Galen with foreboding. The memory of the vikings throwing their goods out of the cart rose up to haunt him as he contemplated their return.

He also worried about Alcuin. He'd said very little about what he'd done during the first viking attack, but Galen had seen a change in his friend. Alcuin was less of the happy-go-lucky man Galen had grown to know and love at the abbey.

He was tense and more irritable than usual, although never towards Galen. Towards him, Alcuin showed deep remorse that made Galen feel guilty. He had given Alcuin no choice about leaving him behind, but his friend was clearly punishing himself for having done it. Nothing Galen said to him could make him feel better.

Worse than that were the nightmares. Alcuin's cries as he tossed about in his sleep had woken Galen more than once. He knew what that was about. Ever since Septimus had attacked him, nightmares had stalked his sleep too.

For Alcuin, it was slightly different. He'd not only had to defend himself against a fearsome enemy, but he'd seen death in battle. From the snatches Galen heard muttered when Alcuin was in the throes of nightmare, he gathered that Alcuin had killed someone.

The two young men acted as each other's confessors now that they were away from the abbey. But Alcuin had so far said nothing to Galen about the death. Maybe that was why it tormented him so much. All Galen could do for Alcuin was pray to God to help him get through it.

'Father thinks the vikings will be back soon,' Albreda said.

Her voice drew Galen back from his dark thoughts and to the realisation that Albreda had arrived and was watching him.

'Does he think so?'

Galen doubted the wisdom of worrying a child over something she could do nothing about.

'We have taken in the harvest. The vikings will want to plunder our stores now, before winter comes.'

Galen realised Albreda was relaying exactly what she'd heard from her father. It was also what Galen knew of the vikings. They spent the autumn out raiding after they'd carried out their own harvest. It was a way of supplementing their stocks and making the most of a quiet time.

Galen wondered whether the lands the vikings came from were particularly harsh, and thus they needed all the things they took by force. Or whether it was greed that drove them on. They certainly seemed to have a great hunger for gold.

'Can you protect us from the vikings?' Albreda asked as she sat down beside Galen and looked up into his face.

Her expression was one of curiosity rather than concern. Galen wished he had her calm assurance.

'I will pray to God to keep us safe,' Galen said.

'And what of your hair? Everyone says the vikings will use it to cast a spell against us.'

'It will do them no good.'

This Galen could say with confidence. Since he wasn't actually a saint, his hair would be of no more use to the vikings than the hair of any other person. There was no point in telling Albreda this, but that was fine, as long as it reassured her.

'Brother Alcuin also said we didn't have to worry because we have the rest of you,' Albreda said with a broad grin.

'Did he?' Galen said dryly.

He understood why Alcuin had said what he'd said. He just wished he hadn't done so. What would they do when the vikings arrived and, God forbid, overran the burh?

Galen offered up yet another heartfelt prayer to God to keep them safe. He wondered if now wasn't the best time to leave the burh. He dismissed the thought the moment he had it.

Alcuin would move them on when he was confident that Galen could travel, and not before. Galen also felt like they had to stay, come what may. They had to offer what protection they could through their prayers. To leave when the townsfolk needed them most would be a heinous act. For the first time, Galen wished he had the saintly powers everyone claimed for him.

The barking of dogs, along with the sound of raised voices at the main gate, drew everybody's attention. The cobbler, Bertwald, dropped the shoe he was working on and ran to investigate, followed by the potter.

'Come on,' Albreda said as she leapt to her feet.

'It would be better if you went and found your mother,' Galen said as he stood up.

He felt shaky with sudden fear, which intensified the pain in his guts. Albreda ignored him and ran in the direction of the gate. Galen watched her go and prayed to God that the commotion wasn't caused by the appearance of vikings. Either way, he had no intention of following the crowd.

He felt like a coward, though, no matter how many times he reassured himself that he was doing the sensible thing. He strained to listen, much like the women who'd emerged from their houses. Some stood in their doorways, while another small group gathered at the end of the square. Their children clung to their skirts and peered in the direction of the noise.

It cut off abruptly. Everyone stood still, waiting. The silence was so profound Galen could hear the birds chirping and wind ruffling the leaves in the trees.

Then Bertwald reappeared.

'They've caught that gleeman, Swidhelm,' he announced to the square. 'Hasculf's going to interrogate him.'

There was a collective murmur of relief. Bertwald picked up his discarded shoe and the women hurried back into their houses. Galen wondered whether Albreda would return, as he sat down and resumed the never-ending task of drinking an entire tankard of beer. It was his duty to do so and necessary if he was to get well enough to resume their journey.

He wondered whether they'd even get out of Wodenshurst alive, but he dismissed that fear immediately. There was no point in dwelling on something he couldn't change. With that heartening thought, he took another big gulp of beer.

'I'm glad to see you are making an effort,' Alcuin said as he arrived from the direction of the main gate.

Galen tilted the mug to show that he was three quarters finished.

'I hear they've captured Swidhelm.'

'News travels fast,' Alcuin said as he came to a stop before Galen and took a deep breath.

He looked like a man who had to discuss something distasteful, which immediately put Galen on alert.

'What is it?'

'Swidhelm has made a curious demand. I hesitate to repeat it.'

'By which I gather it has something to do with me.'

Galen's anxiety rose as Alcuin gave a grave answering nod.

'Swidhelm said he will tell his complete tale, including what he's been doing with the vikings, to one man, and one man only.'

'Me?' Galen gasped.

'I'm afraid so. I suggested to Hasculf that he just beat the information out of Swidhelm. But Hasculf thinks we're more likely to get the truth from the gleeman if we give him what he wants.'

'I see.'

Galen's mind raced to understand the implications of what was being asked of him by both Swidhelm and Hasculf.

'I told him that Swidhelm is most likely just trying to get at you. You are a kind person. He will beg and plead with you to save him and then spin some false tale about what he is up to. I know you are no fool, Galen, but you are very trusting.'

'It isn't for me to decide, though, is it? I merely have to relay what Swidhelm says.'

'There is no hope for him. You know that, don't you?' Alcuin said, fixing Galen with a solemn gaze. 'He is a spy and they will give him no mercy.'

'I know.'

Little as he liked Swidhelm, Galen felt sick knowing he was about to speak to a doomed man. All the same, he had to do what he could for the burh and its people, no matter how queasy it made him feel. He put down the nearly empty mug, unable to stomach the last mouthful.

'There's no sense in putting this off,' Galen said, and pushed himself onto his feet. 'Where is Swidhelm now?'

'He's being held at the main gate,' Alcuin said as he hurried to Galen's right and took his arm to provide extra support.

Galen hoped Alcuin couldn't feel him trembling in his grip. He pulled his left arm up against his body to control the shakes and in reaction to the pain that shot through him as he started walking. That was not something new, but it felt more acute when he was scared, and he was really scared now. He'd never been good at confrontations.

The short walk felt interminable. At the same time, Galen wished it would never end. But it wasn't long before he arrived at the gate.

Hasculf was standing before it, gazing at the ground, his arms crossed over his chest. Odo stood to his right, and another thane, by the name of Cearl, stood on his other side. More men were standing guard on the battlements, their backs to the burh. It reflected how serious the situation was that they didn't even turn to watch as Galen made his slow way up to Hasculf.

'Thank you for doing this,' Hasculf said. 'He's adamant he'll speak to nobody but you, and it may be the quickest way to loosen his tongue. We don't know what he told the vikings or when they'll strike.'

'I will do what I can,' Galen said.

'We have him tied up in the guardroom. He won't be able to touch you. But he said he won't speak unless the two of you are alone.'

'I see.' Galen wished with all his heart that Alcuin could go with him. Since that wasn't possible, he eased his arm out of Alcuin's grip and said, 'You'd best take me to him.'

Hasculf led him the few paces to a solid door set into a small room built under the walkway of the stockade. He pulled the door open and waved his hand for Galen to enter. Inside it was dark, as the only light that entered was via the door and through the gaps in the wooden posts. Swidhelm was on the floor, propped up against the wall. They'd tied his hands in front of him and his feet were tightly bound, so he'd find it difficult to even stand up. His face was bruised, one eye so swollen he couldn't open it, and his lip cut and bleeding.

'They were none too gentle when they captured me,' Swidhelm said, giving Galen a lopsided grin.

'You shouldn't have tried to run,' Hasculf said.

'You can close the door. What I have to say is for the saint's ears alone.'

Galen wanted to beg for the door to remain open, but he couldn't bring himself to speak. He watched as Hasculf closed him into the tiny room with the almost night-like darkness pierced only by a few blades of light. Galen waited until his eyes adjusted to the gloom, then he turned to look at Swidhelm again and was chilled by his expression. He still had the leer, but it was the humourless grin of one who knew he was doomed.

Galen had nowhere to sit, besides the floor. But he doubted he could ease himself down onto it without falling over. So he leaned his back against the wall and hoped his strength would hold out for the duration of the conversation.

'Why... did you want to speak to me?' Galen said. His voice came out soft and shaky.

Swidhelm sighed and gazed up at him, the smile finally banished.

'Are you really a saint?'

'No,' Galen said and took a deep breath to control his increasing anxiety.

'You seem very clear about that.'

'Shouldn't I be the one to know what I am and what I am not?'

'Is that a riddle?'

'I am not a saint.'

Galen wanted no doubt to linger in Swidhelm's mind.

'So what you're saying is that you can't save me?'

'Even if I were a saint, I doubt I could save you. You know the price of betrayal.'

'They will kill me and stick my head on a spike on the path up to the burh,' Swidhelm said. 'I have already been told that.'

'It's what happens to all spies. It's the law. Even if I wanted to change it, I can't.'

'Would you change it if you could? Would you change it for me?'

Galen couldn't understand what Swidhelm was doing. He was afraid that it was all a ploy to delay the inevitable and possibly buy the vikings the time they needed to attack. Although it was midmorning already, and that would be a strange time to start.

'Your question has no meaning. I am not here for a philosophical debate. If that is all you wanted from me, you are wasting time and I will leave you to Hasculf.'

'No, wait!' Swidhelm said and leaned forward. 'I will tell you everything, I swear, if you will do two things for me.'

'What do you want from me?' Galen said, and his unease increased.

'I want you to listen to my confession. It will explain everything. And I want you to get Hasculf to agree to a quick death for me. I can't stand torture.'

'I will ask him.'

Galen was in agreement with both requests. He couldn't stomach torture, no matter what the crime.

'Hasculf will do as you ask,' Swidhelm said. 'He's convinced you are a saint.'

'What is your confession?' Galen said as a wave of dizziness washed over him.

He prayed Swidhelm would keep it short. But as he was facing certain death, he'd want to string out his final moments.

'I was born here, in Enga-lond.'

His first words confirmed Galen's worst fear: Swidhelm was going to stretch this out.

'If you are going to relate your whole life's story, you'd best tell me about the vikings' plans first. I can't risk the lives of everyone in this burh just so you can unburden yourself.'

'Relax, saint,' Swidhelm said and gave another of his lopsided grins. 'We have enough time.'

'How do I know I can trust you about that?'

'The vikings plan to attack tomorrow morning at dawn. You have my word as a Christian. Now you must do what you promised for me.'

'One moment,' Galen said, and banged weakly at the door.

'That was quick,' Hasculf said as he pulled the door open so suddenly that Galen nearly lost his balance.

He had to grab onto Hasculf's tunic to not fall over.

'We have only just started,' Galen said as he straightened himself. 'But Swidhelm tells me the vikings will attack tomorrow at dawn.'

'How will they come? Has he told you that?'

'Patience, Reeve!' Swidhelm said. 'You will get the detail when I have finished what I started with the saint.'

'Would you bring me a stool, please?' Galen said, flushed with embarrassment to make the request.

'Brother Alcuin has already gone to fetch one,' Hasculf said. 'He went off the moment he saw the nature of the guardroom.'

He'd no sooner spoken than Alcuin came running back along the path with the little three-legged folding stool clutched in one hand.

He unfolded it, made sure the leather seat was securely attached and helped Galen to sit before the door was closed on him again.

'So you were born here,' Galen said.

'Aye, a little further south, along this coast,' Swidhelm said. 'My parents, along with the whole hamlet, were Danes who'd settled to make a new life for themselves in this land. It wasn't easy. Your people tried to drive them back into the sea many times. When they weren't being attacked by their neighbours, they were being pillaged by vikings.'

'It sounds like a tough life,' Galen murmured as he curled up into the position that caused him the least pain.

'The life of a churl is never an easy one, and that was what we all were: people scratching a living from the land and the sea. I did the same, and when I grew up, I married a girl from the hamlet and we started a family.'

Galen nodded, certain this tale would not have a happy ending.

'One year, when we had the best supplies we'd ever managed after a rich harvest, the vikings swept in to take the lot. Me and my family included. Well, I didn't want to be sold into slavery, so I fell on my knees and begged them not to do it.

'The viking chieftain laughed and told me my other option was death. But still, I pleaded and told him I would do anything to avoid that dreadful fate. My wife and sons were standing in a huddle of people being loaded onto the boats to become slaves, and they saw it all.

'My wife's expression was indescribable. All the other men had fought bravely and were stoic in their defeat, and here I was on my knees, begging. My wife looked away and covered my children's eyes.'

Galen could see the shame and the pain in Swidhelm's face. He couldn't even imagine what he'd do under the same circumstances. It was better to say nothing, though, and just let the tale unfold. Although he wished it was any tale but this one.

'By fortune, or maybe misfortune, the viking leader said he'd save me if I became a spy for them. He said he'd treat my wife and sons well as long as I kept to my bargain.'

'That was how it started,' Galen murmured.

'From then on I went from hamlet to burh, getting the lie of the land. Early on, I fell in with an old gleeman and supplemented the sagas and poems I had learned as a child with what he taught me. When he died, I inherited his harp and his clothes. People are usually glad to see a gleeman, and it made it easier for me to find out all about them.'

'Which was what you did at the little hamlet of Tiwham, wasn't it?' Galen murmured.

'As with everywhere else. I found their watchmen and told the vikings where they were hidden. In that way, they could be dispatched, and the hamlet burned to the ground before the inhabitants were even aware of it.'

'Many people died there.'

'Their numbers are small compared to all that I have betrayed,' Swidhelm said with a shrug.

'Was it worth it to keep your one life safe?'

'My life, my wife's and that of my sons.'

'Do you think they would thank you for that?'

Galen doubted he could live with himself if he knew it was under such a bargain.

'I don't know. I have never been able to speak to them. Knud, the leader of the vikings who took my family, tells me they are still alive. By now, my sons are grown and probably part of the same viking bands I have been spying for.'

'If that is the case, they have turned into your enemy too.'

'That was one of the reasons I ran away to Wales. But my guilt over my wife and sons brought me back. It was then that Knud said I had to make amends by helping him take Wodenshurst. The first step was to get rid of Tiwham. I think Knud is planning on holding Wodenshurst and using it as a base from which to take even more land.'

'All the more reason to make sure he doesn't succeed,' Galen said, and his stomach constricted in fright.

He was now involved in something more than a mere raid. If the vikings were determined to take the burh, then they were in for a fierce battle indeed.

'Maybe this burh has a better chance of seeing them off than Knud realises.'

'Because it's well guarded?'

'Because it has a saint,' Swidhelm said, back to grinning at Galen.

'And if it doesn't?'

'Maybe just believing it does will give the men sufficient heart to succeed. That small party that raided Tiwham was just preparation. No doubt it annoyed Knud that the men marched to Wodenshurst. All he'd needed was to remove the hamlet quickly and quietly.'

'You must be closer to him than you've led me to believe, if you know that.'

'Knud likes riddles, too. When I met with him last night, I taught him the three you have told the burh and he liked them. For some reason, knowing the riddles made him more certain than ever that you are a holy man. I gained a lot when I gave him your lock of hair.'

'Will he really use it to make a talisman against Wodenshurst?'

'At the very least, he will try to use it to neutralise you.'

Galen nodded. He knew the power of faith, both his and his enemy's. If this Knud thought he had power from the talisman, it would strengthen his resolve.

'Why have you been so forthcoming? Why have you told me all of this? It gains you nothing and puts your family at risk.'

'I am doomed anyway,' Swidhelm said with a shrug. 'If you weren't here, I would have gone to my death spitting and snarling and determined not to say a thing. But with you, I may have some redemption. If you give me your blessing, I have a chink of hope that one day I may be reunited with my family in heaven.'

'I pray you are right.'

'So, will you do it? Will you bless me even though I have sinned?'

'Do you truly repent?' Galen asked. 'Under the eyes of God and His representative on Earth. Do you beg Him for forgiveness for all you have done?'

'I do,' Swidhelm said. 'I really do. God forgive me!'

'Then I bless you,' Galen said, making the sign of the cross over Swidhelm. 'May God have mercy upon your soul.'

CHapter 16

K nowing that the vikings planned to attack, the people of Wodenshurst dropped everything else to prepare for battle.

'Swidhelm may have told you they were coming at dawn,' Hasculf said, 'but we will prepare as if they might attack at any moment.'

Galen nodded acceptance. His long meeting with Swidhelm had drained him emotionally and physically. His further conversation with Hasculf exacerbated this.

Thankfully, the second meeting was held back at the house he and Alcuin used. Alcuin sat silently by his side, providing valuable support, although he did nothing to stop Hasculf's interrogation. They all knew how important it was.

Finally, the reeve had left to oversee preparations, saying as he went, 'We'll gather at dusk and spend the night on the wall. That way no viking will sneak in and take us by surprise.'

'You should rest now,' Alcuin said once they were alone.

'I doubt I can,' Galen said, but didn't resist as Alcuin got him to lie down.

'I feel the same, but the night will be a long one, and we're even less likely to be able to sleep then. We should take the opportunity now so we may be as useful as possible during the battle.'

'Do you intend to fight?' Galen asked and made to sit up again, but Alcuin held him down.

'I will do what I can. Just as at the monasteries where the monks have fought to defend themselves from viking attacks.'

'Even if it causes you to suffer nightmares afterwards?'

'Better that than being overrun and slaughtered.'

Alcuin looked so grim it sent a tremor of fear through Galen.

'Don't you even think about fighting,' Alcuin said.

'I am so weak I doubt I could stand for long enough to even see a viking up close,' Galen said and felt deeply embarrassed to admit it. 'The best I can do for everyone is to pray.'

'Do it in the church. It will give the people courage if they see you at prayer.'

A knock at the door drew both men's attention. Niclas was bobbing up and down before them and wringing his hands.

'I beg your pardon, Master Galen,' he muttered. 'I've told Hasculf that I will join them in this fight. But if you need me for... for protection or anything, I will tell the reeve that I can't help.'

'Protection?' Galen said blankly.

'I could stay by your side and make sure no viking reaches you.'

'It would be better if you were on the battlements,' Alcuin said, 'making sure no viking even gets into the burh. That is a better way to keep Galen safe.'

'He's right.' Galen was aware that Niclas still felt guilty about leaving him behind the first time they had fled the vikings. He also knew that Alcuin had yet to forgive him for it. 'If you keep them away, then none of us will owe the other anything more, not so?'

Niclas gave him a relieved smile.

'I will make sure not a single one of those hairy bastards gets through. You have my word. And with you protecting the burh, we are certain to win.'

Galen sighed to be confronted yet again with the cast-iron conviction that he could protect everyone when he could barely raise a spear. He waved Niclas away, and he took off, relieved to have the permission of his master's son to do what he needed to do.

The power of hierarchy was impressive, Galen thought. His father was absolute master over his people to such an extent that strong men like Niclas deferred even to Hugh's youngest son about what he should do. Their absolute belief in their ealdorman drove them to great heights of bravery. Galen had heard innumerable tales of astonishing heroics accomplished by his father and his men, merely because they had faith in his power and his rank.

He supposed it also made sense that a belief in a saint could provide a boost to the fighting men. It was why they would pray to God and saints before the battle. Just as with his father, Galen realised, the actual outcome of the battle was immaterial. It was the people's state of mind going into it that mattered. He was so afraid of what people would think if he failed to provide them with any protection but, he now saw, that was putting the cart before the horse.

'Do you know,' Galen murmured, staring up into the rafters, 'I don't think I will pray in the church.'

'You won't?' Alcuin said and paused in the process of laying out a sheepskin to sleep on.

'I'm going to be on the battlements with you.'

'Galen! Don't be a fool. It isn't safe.'

'Why should I be tucked away in the church with the old people and the babies while everyone else is fighting?' Galen was aware that his voice was shaking with fear at his foolish bravado, but he meant it. 'If the vikings break in, they will find us and kill us anyway. But I can make a difference on the wall as long as I don't get in anybody's way.'

Galen's determination not to be swayed by anything Alcuin said put paid to any chance either of them had to sleep. Alcuin alternately pleaded and tried to bully Galen into going to the church, or at the very least staying in the old reeve's house.

As the light began to fade, Galen stood up and made his way outside.

'If you think I'm going to help you up onto the wall, you are very much mistaken,' Alcuin snapped.

He pushed past Galen, walking at speed to the gathering point by the wall where the men were due to meet for last-minute instructions.

Galen let him go. He was shaking from the pain in his guts, his fear at what he was about to face, and merely standing up to Alcuin. He didn't think he'd ever done it before, and it came as a shock to both of them.

He hadn't taken more than twenty paces when Alcuin reappeared out of the gloom. He took Galen more roughly than usual by the arm and steered him, without a word, to the gathering place.

'I hear you're joining us on the battlements, Brother Galen,' Hasculf said, looking him up and down.

Galen had never felt more insignificant, but he managed to say, 'If I will not be in your way, I would gladly play my part.'

'You would never be in the way,' Hasculf said as he clapped a heavy hand on Galen's shoulder in welcome. 'There is a spot where you can see over the wall, but it is slightly too far back for the fighters. I usually station one of the boys there to watch the battle and run about with messages. You can keep him company.'

As Hasculf spoke, he tilted his head towards a young lad of about twelve who was the same height and had a similar light build to Galen.

'That's Edric. You're a fortunate boy,' Hasculf said to the youth with the wild sandy hair and a gap between his teeth. 'You get to fight beside a saint.'

The boy grinned and looked at Galen with the kind of awe he'd never experienced before.

'I'd best get up there straight away,' Galen said. 'I'm slow at the best of times.'

'I'll take you up.'

Before Galen could tell him not to, Hasculf hoisted him off his feet, slung him over a shoulder and climbed up the ladder as easily as if he were going up empty-handed.

He put Galen down gently and said, 'I really am glad you'll be with us for this battle.'

Then he turned back to his men and started shouting instructions.

'It's this way, Brother,' Edric said as he arrived on the upper platform after scaling the ladder at speed and bobbed a bow at Galen.

'I'll be beside you too,' Alcuin said as he also came up the ladder.

He'd rammed a simple conical helmet onto his head and then pulled his monk's robe up over the top of it. He had a circular shield with a red and white pattern radiating from the central iron boss on his left arm. He was holding a spear in the other hand. He didn't look remotely like a warrior, despite his athletic build.

'Be careful,' Galen said.

Alcuin laughed.

'If either of us were being careful, we wouldn't be here.'

'Fate sometimes plays strange tricks.'

'Let's hope it is also helpful. Hasculf told me he sent an urgent message to Grantabrycge asking for aid.'

'Are they likely to help?'

'Who knows?' Alcuin said with a shrug. 'They're Danes originally. Hasculf said not to count on their support, so I suppose...'

Galen's slight hope faded with Alcuin's words. He nodded and said as calmly as he could, 'We will manage on our own.'

Alcuin gave him an answering smile and a nod and turned to survey the surrounding countryside.

Galen grasped on to the rough log that formed the wall of the barricade and used it to lower himself to his knees on the platform. He took a deep breath to steady his nerve and looked around. He was at a corner of the fortress, young Edric at his back.

From here he could look down into the burh and its tightly packed collection of houses. Faint lights flickered at many of the windows. It was an unaccustomed sight for this time of night. By now, most people would normally be asleep. But not in this burh tonight.

Every able-bodied man was either already on the barricade, or putting on the last of his armour and on his way there. The old, the infirm and the babies were already at the church, looked after by some of the women. The rest of the women and the older children were at the base of the barricade.

They stood ready to send up supplies of weapons. They were also preparing the fires for the cauldrons of boiling water. These would be tipped down on their enemies when they got close enough. Others were getting ready to take care of the injured. When a burh fought for its existence, everyone took part in the battle.

On the other side of the stockade it was all quiet. Once Galen's eyes adjusted to the darkness, he could make out the grey shapes of the reed beds, some darker blobs of trees and the black curve of the river meandering around the base of the stockade.

There was nothing more for him to do but wait. Galen pulled his hood down low over his face, clasped his hands together and started praying for the safety of the burh. He was dimly aware of the gradual diminution of sound around him as each man found his place and also settled in for a long night of waiting. Nobody slept. They were all far too wound up to even try.

Galen had never been more afraid in his life. In the prayers he was now sending up to heaven, he thanked God for allowing him to grow up in a time when he had faced no serious battles. Certainly none that had made it all the way up to the walls of his home. That reminded him of Willnoth, who had died in a viking raid. He prayed his mother wouldn't lose another son in the same way.

CHAPTER 17

'It's nearly dawn,' Edric murmured into Galen's ear.

Galen stopped mid-prayer and, with the greatest effort, forced his eyes open. It was cold and a faint ribbon of lighter blue was all that he could see on the horizon. The rest still looked like night. But the birds were also aware of the approaching day and had started the first twitters and chirps of the dawn chorus. That was all the vikings would need for a dawn attack. As Galen peered out, he noticed a swirl of lighter grey over the river.

'Is that fog?' Galen whispered.

'It's been building for a while.'

'Will it deter the vikings?' Galen asked, more in hope than expectation.

Edric shrugged, and Galen realised the boy had as much battle experience as he had himself. He squinted down the row of men. They were all standing at the ready along the battlements. Galen sent up another prayer to God to protect them all.

As he prayed, he watched the fog thicken and become more visible as a white blanket in the early dawn light. It seemed to him the fog would help the vikings, as it would keep them invisible as they approached the burh.

'Listen!' Edric hissed.

Galen strained his ears and realised that he could hear rowing over the increasingly raucous birds. Nobody moved around him. Hasculf had warned all the men they had to keep quiet so that the vikings thought their attack would come as a surprise. The plan was to counter-attack at the crucial moment.

Then, out of the gloom and the swirling fog, Galen caught sight of the first longboat. Its high prow with the dragon's head cut a thin line through the mist, followed by the rest of the ship's widening body. It was packed to overflowing with warriors, all heaving at their oars. There was no wind, so the sails had been furled.

'Dear God, protect us,' Galen muttered, as such overwhelming fear gripped him that for a second he could neither breathe nor see.

The first boat was followed by three more, gliding like swans down the river.

'Hold your nerve,' came a whisper along the line of waiting men.

Galen couldn't work out who'd spoken, but it made him hold his breath and his tongue while he continued to send prayers up to heaven.

Then, as the lead ship came into line with the midpoint of the burh, Hasculf bellowed, 'Pull!'

A line of men grabbed on to a thick rope Galen hadn't noticed before and, like men at a tug-o-war, heaved with all their might. Galen couldn't work out what they were doing at first. Then, with another roar, the men pulled again and the rope that snaked over the burh wall lifted. Galen saw that at the end it disappeared into the fog-shrouded water.

Too late, the lead boat realised what was happening as its prow crashed into some unseen barrier.

'That will teach them,' Edric said with satisfaction.

'What is it?' Galen asked.

'It's an iron chain, fixed to the trees on the opposite bank. That viking ship just sailed right into it. With any luck, their boat is now holed and useless to them.'

The men on the wall kept heaving. The boat rocked wildly from side to side, tipping some of the vikings overboard. They vanished with a splash into the mist-shrouded water. A man at the front of the boat was roaring at the rest to regain control.

The following ships were able to come to a stop before they, too, collided with the low-slung chain. They remained side-on to the burh, but the rowers now stood up and started shouting and banging their weapons on their shields. It would have chilled Galen to the bone, were he not already shivering from combined cold and fear. One of the ships unfurled its sail, revealing a spreadeagled raven sewn on to the canvas.

'That's a message to us,' Edric gasped, 'that they'll leave nothing but bodies for the ravens to feast on after this battle.'

As if that weren't bad enough, a man dressed in the most impressive armour Galen had ever seen, with a bearskin for a cape, shouted for quiet. His men abruptly ceased their jeers. The chieftain gestured for an old man to step forward.

'It's one of their priests,' Edric said, and he sounded more frightened than he had till now.

And well he should, Galen thought. The man may have been old, but he was as tough and sinewy as all the other warriors. He'd painted his face with unfamiliar black symbols and he had a necklace of bones and massive claws that looked terrifying.

'You think your saint will protect you, worms?' the viking chief shouted in his thick, hard-to-understand Danish, as he gestured to his priest.

The old man held up a leather pouch, etched with white runes. He tossed it into the air, accompanied by a chant that Galen couldn't understand. It burst into ruddy flames that drew a gasp from the men on both sides who watched as it burnt out, the smouldering embers drifting down and vanishing into the mist.

'It's a curse,' Alcuin muttered from Edric's other side.

'That is what we have done to your saint's hair. And that is what we will do to your saint when we catch him,' the viking chief roared.

'Go back, Knud, you may have stolen some hair from our saint, but he will protect this burh. You will gain nothing from today,' Hasculf shouted back.

'Quickly, Edric, help me up,' Galen gasped, and held out his hand.

'Are you sure?' Edric said.

'Now!'

Galen struggled to get himself up because his legs had gone numb from kneeling all night while he prayed.

'Alright,' Edric said and pulled so hard on Galen that he went flying forward and crashed into the wall.

Galen blinked away the tears of pain that the bump forced out of him. He'd meant to shout a blessing, but he could no longer speak. All he could do was make a sign of the cross over the men of the burh. A thunderous clap of wings drew everyone's attention to the copse of trees opposite as a multitude of honking ravens took to the skies and circled overhead.

'Flee now, Knud,' Hasculf said, eyeing the big, black, wheeling birds with satisfaction. 'While you still have a chance.'

'Never! We have come for this burh and we will take it before the day is over,' Knud roared and threw his spear at Hasculf. It pegged into the wall a man's body-length from the top.

The rest of the vikings also heaved their spears. The stockade trembled with the force of the impact as some spears bit and others clattered to the ground below.

'Hold!' Hasculf shouted to his men.

Spears were too precious to throw before they could do proper damage. The last thing Hasculf wanted was to provision his enemy. The vikings pulled their boats nearer to the bank's edge and the men swarmed out over the sides. Some vanished, dropping like stones into the inky depths of the river, dragged down by the weight of their armour and weapons.

'We deepened it,' Edric said with satisfaction. 'They thought they were leaping into shallow water, but they were wrong.'

Unfortunately, the vikings realised the risk and heaved the boats right to the river's edge before the rest leapt across to dry land. Then, with a roar, they ran up the steep earthen side of the barricade. They jumped for the pegged spears and used them as ladders up the wall.

'Now!' Hasculf shouted.

The men of Wodenshurst launched a volley of spears down onto the heads of the swarming raiders, while the group that had been holding the rope hacked it off, so it fell down and away and the vikings couldn't climb it. The vikings held their shields overhead for protection against the raining weapons. The women of Wodenshurst handed up cauldrons of boiling water that the men tipped over the enemy.

Galen shuddered at the shrieks of the scalded and wounded, and the shouts and grunts of the fighters. He sank back to his knees and prayed.

Galen kept his eyes closed as the battle raged about him. He was so focused on his prayers that he barely registered anything else. The pain in his guts and his legs increased, but that scarcely mattered. The sun rose and burned away the mist, and Galen was dimly aware of sweat trickling down his back. Still, he kept his head bowed and his prayers going up to heaven.

He only looked up once, when he heard Alcuin shout, 'Galen, for the love of God!'

Galen's head jerked up, and his eyes flew open at the moment a viking's face appeared, leering over the sharpened stakes of the stockade. The man aimed a spear at Galen and threw it just as Alcuin brought his shield down on the man's head and he vanished with an abrupt yell.

Galen blinked at the spear that landed at his feet as if it were an unfathomable riddle. Then he shook his head. The spear didn't matter. Edric had vanished. Galen hoped he was merely on an errand. There were fewer men on the battlements now, and they looked more frantic.

Galen sank back into the only thing he could do and continued praying. He wasn't sure how many more hours passed. A detached part of him noticed the gradual diminution of the sounds of battle.

There was less shouting now. The men had run out of energy. All they had left was grim determination. For the men of Wodenshurst, it was to keep themselves and their families safe. For the vikings, it was a determination to take and hold a new home.

Somewhere, a fatally wounded man was keening his last. It was a shrill shriek that Galen had seldom heard and wished he could wipe from his memory. Then another sound came to his ears. The call of a hunting horn.

Its mournful tone sounded like it was coming from outside. To Galen's surprise, the men in the burh started cheering. Galen forced his eyes open and spotted Edric, sunburned, smudged with ash, and with a trickle of blood running down the side of his temple. He looked elated, his eyes shining in victory.

'They've come,' Edric shouted, jumping up and down in excitement. 'The men of Grantabrycge have come to our aid!'

'Thank God,' Galen muttered, but he was incapable of moving.

He was so exhausted he didn't even want to stand up and survey this relieving army. Instead, he searched for Alcuin. He, too, looked exhausted. His face was white with strain, and sweat formed rivulets through the dust on his cheeks. He kept an eye over the wall, but the rest of him was straining to see the new men.

Another blast of the horn rang out and the men on the wall turned to their foes and rained the last of their weapons down onto their heads.

'They're running,' Edric said with satisfaction as he risked a look over the wall himself. 'They can't defeat us with the addition of the men of Grantabrycge.'

Galen gave him a relieved nod and offered up a prayer of gratitude-filled thanks to God for saving the burh.

'Do you want to see?' Edric asked.

'I'll help too,' Alcuin said.

'Are you alright?' Galen murmured, because the pallor of Alcuin's face alarmed him.

'I don't have a scratch on me,' Alcuin said, forcing a smile that did nothing to reassure Galen.

Still, he was grateful to have the help of Edric and Alcuin. Even though the pain of straightening his legs was excruciating, he wanted to see what was going on.

His first thought was that it was later than he realised. It seemed to be late afternoon. The men of the burh were now hanging over the battlements, shouting and banging anything they had to hand. The vikings were fleeing to their remaining boats. The lead boat looked half sunk now. Its prow was barely visible above the ripples of the river, the stern was far too high in the air.

The injured vikings were dragged onto their boats by the scruff of their necks or even by their hair. The moment the men were all aboard, the boats cast off and they rowed them away. The men of Grantabrycge, fresh and clean with not a scratch on them, rushed to the water's edge. They shouted for the vikings to come back and see what they made of some real fighters.

'That's quite a band of thanes,' Alcuin murmured of the newly arrived warriors.

'They got here in the nick of time,' Hasculf said as he strolled over.

Galen had watched his approach. He'd gone from man to man on the barricade, giving them all a pat on the back and a hearty, encouraging word.

'You weren't sure they'd come at all.'

'No, and now we'll have to welcome them in and feed them for their trouble. I suppose I shouldn't complain, though. Their arrival ended the battle and I am grateful for that.'

'Do you think you could have done it without them?'

'With you on our side, Brother Galen,' Hasculf said, giving him a thorough back pounding, 'I was certain we'd win, and I wasn't wrong.'

Galen gave him a weak smile and said, 'I think the men of Grantabrycge would disagree. But I'd like to ask you for a favour. Please don't tell these newcomers about me.'

'Whyever not?' Hasculf said, and looked as astonished as he sounded.

'Just don't, please,' Galen said.

'If that is what you wish, then I will do it. But I can't understand your reason.'

'I would prefer not to make a fuss, that's all,' Galen said and looked to Alcuin.

He was feeling faint. He hoped Alcuin would come to his rescue, although his friend looked just as shaken and in need of support as he was today.

Thankfully, Alcuin understood and said, 'I will get Galen back to our house so he can rest. We'll stay there while the men of Grantabrycge are about.'

Hasculf gave an accepting, if reluctant, nod.

'In the meantime, I need to greet our newly arrived guests and see to my people. Edric, you help the brothers.'

Edric swelled with pride to be given such an important task, which brought a smile to Galen's face despite everything else.

CHAPTER 18

It took Galen and the residents of the burh a few days to get over their ordeal. During that time, Galen and Alcuin stayed in their hut, caught up on their sleep and spent more time than was usual in prayer. Alcuin also did a full confession to Galen. He finally mentioned the man he'd killed, along with talking about the pain and terror of the latest battle.

'Thank God I'm not a warrior,' Alcuin said, making light of his feelings. 'I don't have the ruthlessness needed for it.'

'I think it's something you gain over time,' Galen murmured. 'But I, too, am glad that neither one of us will have to grow accustomed. You might have the body of a warrior, but I don't even have that.'

'You have more than enough.'

Since it was Alcuin's confession and Galen didn't want Alcuin to tell him he was braver than he thought, he waved away the comment. Instead, he gave Alcuin the standard blessing at the end of a confession.

Alcuin got up off his knees with a relieved sigh and brushed his robe clean.

'Hasculf tells me that the ealdorman of Grantabrycge and his men have finally left. He thinks he managed to keep all mention of you and me from their ears.'

'That's good.'

'The burh has also settled down again. They have buried the dead, and most of the injured have recovered enough to go back to work. Many of the refugees have also returned to their hamlets.'

'Don't they believe the vikings will come back?'

Galen thought it was a distinct possibility.

'Hasculf says they will always be ready for an attack,' Alcuin said, 'but that winter is almost upon us, and the vikings will not wish to risk sailing in stormy weather. Besides, after the drubbing they got here, they'll stay away for a while.'

'I am relieved to hear it.'

'And now lunch,' Alcuin said, brightening considerably as Ivetta appeared at their door with a tray of food.

'I see you are recovered,' Ivetta said, smiling warmly at them. 'This is the most cheerful either of you has been so far.'

'How is everyone else?' Galen asked.

'They are doing remarkably well, I'm happy to say.'

'That is a relief. I wonder...' Galen was uncertain of how to say what he needed to without putting anyone on the defensive. 'Are you still using the charms, Madam Ivetta?'

Ivetta coloured and said, 'I know you don't like them, but they really do help our injured men.'

'Actually, I was going to offer to copy out a few more for you. When I read the charms you'd put up around this house, well, there were lots of mistakes in them. I can rewrite them so they are correct again.'

'And there you see the real Galen,' Alcuin said with a laugh. 'No doubt he has been itching to correct your charms from the moment he saw them.'

'Is that why you didn't like them, because they are badly written?' Ivetta said, looking relieved. 'I thought you disapproved.'

Galen decided against saying one way or another what he really thought of the charms. He'd learned from his stay in Wodenshurst that perception was every bit as important as reality. Galen had seen how heartened the men were to have him on the wall with them, even though he was useless as a fighter. He knew that everyone in the burh put great stock in the charms as well. So the least he could do was make sure they were copied correctly.

'Albreda tells me she already knows all the charms by heart. Do you think she'd be willing to help me decipher what should be written on each of them?'

'Willing?' Ivetta said with a laugh. 'She'd be thrilled. But where will you get the parchment for these rewritten charms? I can give you some, but I don't have much.'

'I've cut up the pages the vikings damaged when they pillaged our cart. There is enough there for the burh's needs.'

'But what of the king's book? I thought your parchment was meant for him.'

'We will have to replenish our supplies when we reach Lundenburh,' Alcuin said. 'These sheets really aren't useable for the king's book anymore.'

'You are both very kind,' Ivetta said. 'Because of that, I hesitate to make my next request. But will you please write that you made these charms on the back of each sheet?'

'Me?' Galen said. 'Why do you need that?'

Ivetta flushed bright red and said, 'That way we'll know which are the correct ones.'

Galen suspected there was more to the request than that. He feared it was because of the burh's firm belief that he was a saint. But as he didn't want to talk about that, he nodded and said, 'I will do as you ask.'

Alcuin lay in bed and took a deep, contented sniff of the morning air. It was fragrant with woodsmoke and the cool scent of the surrounding marshland. Winter was nearly upon them. It was time to continue their journey.

Alcuin felt considerably better for his rest. He'd been exhausted after the battle. His arms and legs were so tired that they shook, but it was his heart that had suffered the most from the brutality of war.

He looked around for Galen and found him where he always was these days: at a low table by the open door. He was scratching away with his pen at the charms for the burh. Alcuin sensed Galen was putting as many prayers as he could into the strips of parchment, because his lips moved as he wrote. Galen feared for the safety of the burh and was doing everything he could to ensure its survival even after they left.

Alcuin was seeing a new side to Galen during their journey. He was a shy man, no doubt about it. But if people were kind to him, he loved them back without question. Alcuin realised Galen was the same towards him, unquestioning in his loyalty and affection. It was a dangerous trait for a grown man.

In many ways, Galen resembled the ever-present Albreda. She looked up to Galen and saw only good. That was fair enough. Galen wasn't only copying out the charms for the burh, but also teaching Albreda letters and reading as he did so. It seemed his hope was that Albreda would continue to produce literate charms long after he was gone.

Galen must have sensed that he was being watched, because he looked up and smiled at Alcuin.

'You think it's time to go, don't you?'

Alcuin sighed and gave a nod.

'You've walked right around the burh two days in a row. And you've also, finally, put on weight. I've never seen your cheeks with such a natural colour.'

'I do feel better than I have for a long time. And despite not being important enough for the king to worry about, I don't want to keep him waiting any longer.'

Alcuin laughed. He knew Galen had been worrying nonstop about the king, but biting his tongue and waiting for Alcuin to decide.

'I've had Niclas ride out in search of travelling companions. Hasculf has said it would be better for us to go to Lundenburh in a group. Niclas has come across a band of pilgrims who should be here by tomorrow. They're all walking, so their speed will suit us too.'

'Tomorrow,' Galen murmured and looked out into the little square. 'I shall miss this place.'

'As will I. They have been very kind and welcoming. But I hope our stay here has also shown you that you are fine with strangers.'

Galen might have countered that comment, but Albreda arrived, beaming at them.

'Are you ready for your walk, Brother Galen?'

'I am indeed,' Galen said and pushed himself to his feet.

No matter how much better he got, he was still in pain and moved slowly and carefully.

'Today I will leave Galen entirely in your care,' Alcuin said, giving Albreda a meaningful stare. 'Make sure he doesn't overdo his exercise.'

'You can rely upon me, Brother Alcuin.'

Albreda looked even prouder of her extra responsibility. Alcuin had his doubts. Albreda always accompanied him and Galen on their walks these days.

But as a typical child, she didn't keep pace with them. She'd dash ahead, then return to show them things or point out items of interest. Then she'd lag behind for a chat with some friend or another before rejoining them again. But he supposed with her and Galen combined, they'd be fine.

'Where are you going?' Albreda asked.

'I need to have a word with your father.'

Alcuin waited only long enough to see Galen and Albreda off before he headed for the main gate. It was the most likely place to find Hasculf. He was talking to Odo and Cearl and young Edric as they surveyed the battlements and discussed repairs and extra fortifications.

The men spotted Alcuin before Hasculf did and gave him a nod which drew the reeve's attention.

'Ah, Brother Alcuin, what can I do for you?' Hasculf said, while the others backed away out of earshot.

'Niclas has found a band of pilgrims for us to join. It's time we set off back on our travels.'

'I thought that might be the case. Then we will have to hold a farewell feast for you.'

'There really is no need for that. You have fed and housed three of us and our mules for an unconscionably long time.'

'Nonsense. Brother Galen did far more for me and Ivetta when he rescued little Albreda. Not to mention holding back the viking horde. Besides, we have another favour to ask of him.'

'Have you? Well then, you'd best speak to him.'

'Actually,' Hasculf said, looking embarrassed for the first time and pulling at the golden torque around his neck, 'I was hoping you'd speak to him for us.'

'Us? Who exactly?'

'The whole burh.'

'What do you want?'

Alcuin was now on guard against what the burh might ask. He hoped he could turn off any inappropriate request without causing offence.

'Well,' Hasculf said, shifting from one foot to the other, 'we'd be grateful if Brother Galen would bless each of the children in the burh.'

'All of them? They surely can't all want a miracle.'

'No, of course not, but... well, what harm can it do? And if good comes of it... so much the better.'

'Brother Galen is a very modest man. This request will embarrass him.'

'That's why we were hoping you would talk to him for us. We don't want him to feel beholden but... we'd be eternally grateful.'

Alcuin sighed and said, 'Alright, I'll ask him, but don't get your hopes up.'

'No, of course not,' Hasculf said with a relieved laugh. 'Thank you, Brother Alcuin.'

Alcuin gave a slight nod and then realised that rather a lot of the townsfolk were standing about. They were listening in, waiting to see what the outcome of Hasculf's request would be. Then he wondered what Galen would say. Knowing his friend, he'd probably agree to the request. But at the same time, he'd feel uncomfortable about it.

Alcuin wasn't keen either. To give himself some time to consider the problem, he set off on his own circuit of the burh. He thought he might catch up with Galen and Albreda as he walked.

In the event, he was so lost in thought he slowed to a snail's pace and only caught up with Galen when he got back to their hut. Galen was seated on the little bench, soaking in the sun. He smiled as Alcuin approached and pointed at a half-drunk mug of beer.

'See, I'm still following orders.'

'And I'm glad of it,' Alcuin said, noting that Albreda was no longer about. 'Now I have a rather odd request to make of you, and if we are to have any privacy in this discussion, we'd better go inside.'

'Really?' Galen said, and his eyes darted around the burh.

He must have noticed the people watching the two of them. So he got up and walked in the slow, measured and slightly hunched posture that caused him the least pain, into the hut.

'What is going on?'

'They want to you bless all their children.'

'Really?'

'You seem less surprised than I expected.'

'I've sensed a couple of people wanted to ask me before. And, strangely enough, Cwengyth asked it of me too. She said others would make the same request, although she didn't explain why.'

'Well, I think it has something to do with the miracle here.'

'Yes, it was bound to. But these people have been very kind to us, so it is the least I can do for them.'

'I'm glad you see it that way,' Alcuin said. 'It's rather irregular, but it is what they want.'

CHapter 19

Galen settled back on the bench outside the hut before the farewell banquet in their honour. Then the children and their parents queued up in an expectant, hushed row that snaked down the lane. Alcuin stood by Galen's side to offer him moral support. He was struck by the fact that all the children had been cleaned and dressed in their best clothes. It was as though this was the most important event in their little lives.

'Well,' Galen said, looking overwhelmed by all the attention, 'who wants to be first?'

'Me,' Albreda said. 'Brother Galen is my friend, aren't you? You've taught me lots of riddles and how to read and write.'

'I suppose I have,' Galen said.

Alcuin couldn't suppress a grin at this outspoken little girl's assumptions. Galen wouldn't have been able to repudiate her even if he'd wanted to. She'd practically taken up residence with him during the day.

Galen put his hand over her forehead and said, 'Oh Lord, bless this child, Albreda. Keep her safe and in health and always within the loving embrace of her family.'

Albreda grinned at him whilst Hasculf and Ivetta beamed with pride. Albreda took up a position beside

Galen. She evidently didn't intend to go anywhere, as she saw herself in the light of a deputy.

Galen continued his blessings, from tall, strapping boys who towered over him and had to kneel for him to reach them, to babies in arms. For each one, he said something different, personal and meaningful. Alcuin swelled with pride to know this man who cared so deeply about people. He took the time to say something special to each of them in a language they could all understand, rather than muttering the same Latin blessing for each child.

'Well, that's the last,' Galen said of chubby Hengist of the long sleeves.

He grinned, then pushed his brother Edric, who'd laughed at the blessing he'd got.

'Which means it's time for the feast!' Hasculf said, rubbing his hands together enthusiastically. 'And I'd say you've earned it, Brother Galen. Double helpings of meat for you tonight, I can tell you.'

'I can't even finish your single helpings,' Galen said with a laugh. 'You're far too generous, Hasculf.'

'Nonsense! There's no such thing.'

The festivities went on well into the night. Alcuin thought it was as well the pilgrims were only due to arrive around midmorning. Otherwise, he'd have had to hustle Galen out of the party way too early. Now, he left Galen to enjoy himself, soaking up the warm atmosphere and the friendly faces around him. Alcuin was all too aware that the palace

wouldn't be as accepting a place. So he didn't have the
heart to take Galen away till he really started looking
tired.

'It's time, my lords,' Niclas said, poking his head
through the door. 'The pilgrims are an hour away from
Wodenshurst.'

His words sent a quiver of fear through Galen, who'd
been slowly waking up after a rather long night of
feasting. Their stay was over and they would shortly be
back on the road to Lundenburh.

'It looks late.'

Alcuin sat up in his bed and said, 'There was no reason
to get up before we had to, but now we'd best hurry.'

There wasn't much to do, really. Alcuin and Niclas
had packed the cart the night before. It had lost about a
third of its load, but Alcuin was confident that the king
could replace anything the vikings had taken.

'For,' he said, as Galen tied up his little bundle of
goods, 'he is sure to have more gold leaf than even the
abbey.'

That was probably true. Now Galen pulled up his
hood and took a last look at the hut. Then he turned
and gave an accepting nod to Alcuin.

They stepped out into the little square and Galen
realised that it was silent and empty.

'Where have they all gone?'

'My guess is the main gate,' Alcuin said.

'Aye, word got around that we were about to leave the moment I got back,' Niclas said. 'That Odo has quite the tongue on him. He can't keep a secret.'

'That's rich coming from you,' Alcuin said, but his laugh took the sting out of his words.

He took Galen's arm and supported him in his usual way. Despite the warmth and kindness the people of Wodenshurst had shown him, it still surprised Galen to see the crowd waiting to bid them a safe journey.

'I'm glad you're travelling in a bigger company now,' Hasculf said as he stood at the head of that group with Ivetta and Albreda. 'These are dangerous times and there is safety in numbers. Especially when journeying to Lundenburh. It's a whole other type of bandit you have to watch out for around the outskirts of that city.'

'We'll keep a wary eye open. Thank you, Hasculf, and thanks once again for your hospitality,' Alcuin said.

'You and Brother Galen can always be certain of a welcome here,' Hasculf said as he shook both men by the hand.

'We have grown so used to having you here that I fear we will miss you greatly,' Ivetta said. 'I don't even know what Albreda will do without you, Brother Galen.'

'She'll be fine,' Galen said, and felt his face flush.

'But I will miss you, Brother Galen,' Albreda said and flung her arms around his waist.

'Albreda don't! You know you're not allowed to touch monks,' Ivetta said. 'I'm sorry, Brother Galen, she young and unmindful.'

'It's alright,' Galen said. 'Our order isn't so strict that it can't look with benevolence upon a kind act.'

'We will miss you!' Ivetta said with passion.

Then she took her daughter and pulled her back into the crowd.

'Aye, she speaks for us all,' Hasculf said as he helped Alcuin get Galen into the cart and waved them on their way.

Galen watched the people gathered around the burh's entrance, waving as the cart rolled slowly down the road. Wodenshurst had been a place of turmoil and war, but he was still sorry to be leaving. Galen pulled himself upright on his cushions and tried to look around the cart to see the band of pilgrims they'd be joining. He couldn't see them yet, but he prayed they would ensure a less eventful trip to Lundenburh than they'd had so far.

The thought of arriving at the king's hall unsettled Galen. It would be an altogether different ordeal, and one he wasn't sure he was ready for.

Enjoyed this book?

If you are like me, you use reviews to decide whether you want to buy a book. So if you enjoyed the book, please take a moment to let people know why. The review can be as short as you like.

Thank you very much!

CHAPTER 20

BACKGROUND TO THE BOOK

I have tried to be historically accurate, but looking back that far is difficult and can always only be a guess. The clothes, food, medicines and ranks, and daily and religious life, are as close as my historical research permits.

At the time, the British Isles was a feudal society subdivided amongst several warring kingdoms, although England had been unified by Aethelstan in 927AD. In addition, Danes were alternately trading, attempting to settle and raiding all along the coast. Vikings were pirates. If the people were trading peacefully, they were called Danes, if they were raiding, they were called vikings, but they were often the same people. Because I am using the term viking to refer to pirates, rather than to a people, I have not capitalised the word.

This book starts in the late summer of 997 AD in Anglo-Saxon England, or Enga-lond as it was known then. The towns and villages I mention are my own invention and never existed except for Grantabrycge, which is modern-day Cambridge, and Lundenburh, which is modern-day London. England at that time was very different and much marshier. It has since been extensively drained.

CHAPTER 21

GLOSSARY

Burh: fortified town or village.

Churl: a freeman of the lowest rank; a peasant.

Ealdorman: nobility; this became the modern-day earl.

Enga-lond: the Anglo-Saxon name for England.

Englisc: the Anglo-Saxon word for English.

Habit: the clothes a monk wears. A habit consists of a tunic (plain, single piece robe), a scapular (a garment that hangs from the shoulders but has no arms) and a cowl/hood (a long, single piece garment with a hood and wide sleeves which fits over the top of the tunic and scapular).

Ham/hamlet: small village.

Infirmarius: a monk who looked after the sick monks and any poor people who needed medical attention.

Grantabrycge: the Anglo-Saxon name for Cambridge.

Leech: a doctor. While for us leech may be a derogatory term, in the Anglo-Saxon era it was merely the name of their occupation because they used leeches for treatment.

Lundenburh: the Anglo-Saxon name for London.

Mint: place where money is made. That money was silver pennies. During Anglo-Saxon times, most major towns had their own mint.

Parchment: a kind of durable paper made from the skins

of animals, usually pigs, sheep or goats.

Shire: an administrative district.

Shire Reeve: what was later to become the sheriff. His role was to supervise the shires, just as the port reeve supervised ports and the market reeve managed the markets. He was an estate manager to more powerful men such as ealdormen and local bishops, and in some cases reporting directly to the king. Part of their role was to collect taxes and maintain law and order, including adjudicating over trials.

Thane: a warrior; what was to become a knight in later centuries.

Thrall: a slave. People might be forced into slavery when they fell upon hard times. Then they could offer their labour to someone wealthy or powerful in exchange for their freedom. This was usually described as putting your head into somebody else's hands.

Vellum: a high-quality parchment usually made from calfskin.

Vikings: the term used for pirates. The word itself is assumed to mean either sea robber or sea trader.

Wealisc: the Welsh, although the literal translation of the word from Anglo-Saxon means 'foreign'.

GET ALL MY SHORT STORIES FOR FREE!

Building a relationship with my readers is one of the great things about being a writer. That is why I continue to upload a wide collection of short stories for free on my website. These currently include a collection of short stories, and some individual longer short stories including a Galen spin off, a quirky tale about a rabbit in Lisbon and a couple of Christmas romances.

Sign up for my no-spam newsletter that only goes out when there is a new book or freebie available, at: www.marinapacheco.me

ALSO BY

Get all my books here:

MEDIEVAL HISTORICAL FICTION ePub, paperback and hardback
Fraternity of Brothers, *Life of Galen, Book 1* – Cast out for a crime committed against him, his future looks bleak. Until an unexpected visitor gives him hope for justice. A fight for acceptance, absolution and friendship in Anglo-Saxon England.
Comfort of Home, *Life of Galen, Book 2* – Proven innocent, he's returned from exile. Can he recover all that he lost? A tale of friendship and return to a family he thought he'd lost, set in Anglo-Saxon England.
Kindness of Strangers, *Life of Galen, Book 3* – Trapped in a land plagued by vikings, can one small miracle be all they need to survive? A tale of miracles, betrayal and friendship while under viking siege.
The King's Hall, *Life of Galen, Book 4* – As if

being commissioned to create a book to turn back the Apocalypse isn't enough, intrigue and romance threaten to destroy everything he's come to rely upon. Friendship, love and intrigue at the court of King Aethelred the Unready.

Restless Sea, *Life of Galen, Book 5* – Just when they thought they could go home, they're thrust into an adventure at sea. A journey that tests the bonds of friendship.

Friend of My Enemy, *Life of Galen, Book 6* – Captured by an implacable enemy, their future looks bleak. Will escape even be possible?

Road to Rome, *Life of Galen, Book 7* — A journey across a turbulent continent. Will Galen find the answers he seeks?

Eternal City, *Life of Galen, Book 8* — Galen and Alcuin delve into the secrets of the corrupt and decaying city of Medieval Rome.

AUDIOBOOKS narrated by Jacob Daniels
Fraternity of Brothers, *Life of Galen, Book 1*
Comfort of Home, *Life of Galen, Book 2*
Kindness of Strangers, *Life of Galen, Book 3*
The King's Hall, *Life of Galen, Book 4*
   Restless Sea, *Life of Galen, Book 5*

HISTORICAL ROMANCE: ePub, paperback, hardback and audiobooks with AI narration
Sanctuary, *a sweet Medieval mystery* – He needs shelter.

She wants a way out. Will his brave move to protect risk both their hearts? An optimistic tale of redemption with heart-warming characters and feel-good thrills.

The Duke's Heart, *a sweet Victorian romance* – His body may be weak, but his dreams know no bounds. Will she be the answer to his prayers? A disabled duke, a strong and determined woman and a slow-building relationship.

Duchess in Flight, *a swashbuckling romance* – She's on the run from a deadly enemy. He lives in the shadows of truth. When their lives merge, will their battle for survival lead to love? A reluctant hero, a woman and her children in distress, a chase to the death.

What the Pauper Did, *a body swap mystery romance* – How do you define yourself? Is it through your appearance, your memories or your soul? Intrigue, murder and romance in an alternate Lisbon of 1770.

CONTEMPORARY ROMANCE ePub, paperback, hardback and audiobooks with AI narration
Scent of Love – Can two polar opposite perfumers overcome their differences and create a unique blend all of their own? Love, intrigue and clashing values in the perfume houses of Lisbon.

Sky Therapy — A detective and the son of a serial killer. Is it safest to stay apart, or will they risk everything for love?

SCIENCE FICTION/ FANTASY ePub and paperback
City of Night, *Eternal City, Book 1* – World-threatening danger, a female demonologist, an unwitting apprentice, a city in a single tower, a satisfying ending.

SHORT STORIES: ePub, paperback, and AI narration
Living, Loving, Longing, Lisbon, Vol 1 & Vol 2 – A collection of short stories inspired by the city of Lisbon, written by people from around the world who live in, visited or love Lisbon.
Loves of Lisbon – An advent calendar of 24 short, sweet romances of the intertwining lives of the residents of Lisbon.

FREEBIES: ePub and AI narration
Shorties – My shortest works: futuristic, contemporary and historical.
White Rabbit of Lisbon – A whimsical short story. What will happen when a rabbit and a raven fall in love?
Scourge of Demons – How would you deal with your demons? A short story set in the world of the Life of Galen series.
The Greek Gift – A Christmas short story. At the gym he ignored her; will it be any different at the Christmas Eve party?
Christmas Fates – A Christmas short story. Aurora Dawn is about to learn the true meaning of Christmas

and it has nothing to do with how many of the latest must-haves she can sell.

ABOUT AUTHOr

Marina Pacheco a binge writer of historical fiction, sweet romance, sci-fi and fantasy novels as well as short stories. She writes easy reading, feel-good novels that are perfect for a commute or to curl up with on a rainy day. She currently lives on the coast just outside Lisbon, after stints in London, Johannesburg, and Bangkok, which all sounds more glamorous than it actually was. Her ambition is to publish 100 books. This is taking considerably longer than she'd anticipated!

You can find out more about Marina Pacheco's work, and download several freebies, on her website: https://marinapacheco.me
Website: https://marinapacheco.me
   Sign up to Marina's newsletter via her website or on Substack to keep up to date on all her writing activities, get early previews of covers and first chapters, short stories and freebies.
Follow me on substack:
https://substack.com/@marinapacheco
email: hi@marinapacheco.me

Printed in Great Britain
by Amazon

61056594R10109